MADAM PRESIDENT

AND OTHERS

MARY JACQUELINE PINCH

PublishAmerica
Baltimore

Softcover 9781627099523
PUBLISHED BY PUBLISHAMERICA, LLLP
www.publishamerica.com
Baltimore

Printed in the United States of America

DEDICATION

This book is dedicated to Mary Suzanne Pebworth McKinney, my daughter, my constant caregiver, and my friend.

This book is also dedicated to Nina Annette Pebworth Huff, my daughter, my dedicated editor, and my friend.

CONTENTS

MADAM PRESIDENT

AND OTHERS

MADAM PRESIDENT

Roy came rushing into the kitchen so fast that he had to hold onto the wall for a minute before he could speak. Dottie knew where he had gone, to hear the new president's speech at the inauguration, and he was so excited that she could tell he had been crying. The news would be *good* for a change. The people had voted to let the presidents stay in office for a term of ten years, beginning with this one, and had elected the most non-political, who gives-a-rat's –ass about a murderer having civil rights, just down-right hardcore woman, who said everybody was going to work, and she meant *everybody*. She told the multitudes that they had better not put her in office unless they were dead serious about cleaning up America and making it a good, strong country where people were proud to be Americans, their children could play safely in the yard or walk to school. She had warned the deadbeats that they would be seeing her soon. Very soon. Poor Roy had spit all his words out so fast that he just slumped down in a chair, put his head on Dottie's arm, and cried.

At 24, Roy had married Dottie, who was 23. They had been sweethearts since grade school, and were now working toward their happy dream of good jobs, a nice little home, children, and lots of love throughout their lifetimes. They were always content with the simple things in life, but they were not to get even a little of their dreams. Exactly one month after they got their first small apartment, and began their jobs, Roy was laid off due to cutbacks. A week later Dottie joined him in the unemployment lines. They found out very quickly that food stamps and an unemployment check did little to pay the rent and utilities. They lost the apartment and went to live in the over-the-garage apartment that Roy's parents had kept for relatives to use when they visited. In exchange for the apartment, they did everything in their power to ease life for Roy's parents. They kept up the yard, grew vegetables, raised chickens, and even sold some of the eggs when there was abundance.

Today, for the very first time in two years, Roy was a happy man, and Dottie did not seem as haggard as usual while she listened to him talk about the future. Presidents had come and gone with their promises, but for some reason, this woman seemed to be just like every other American who was sick of flowery speeches and hollow promises that disappeared five minutes after inauguration. She told the masses that there would be absolutely *no* lavish parties in the White House, at the citizens' expense, *no* vacations, at their expense, and to be ready, to begin going back to work in one month. She warned that the jobs might not be exactly what each wanted, but a job was a job if it brought money into the family. She warned that she would not tolerate one single word about equal opportunities, women's rights, men's rights, race, religion, or any damn thing that would delay Americans going back to work. She made it clear that anyone causing any trouble or getting in the way of the workers would be jailed. *PERIOD!*

As promised, one month, to the day, Maude Rugsby sat down at her desk, in the Oval Office, ready to incite America. If they never had anything else to give them all hope, this would be the start and there was plenty more to come.

"Madam President, we go live in 5-4-3-2-GO!" John, the cameraman, was so excited that he was having trouble not fainting. Imagine being the very first guy in America, to film the very first ten-year president, on her very first speech. Gathering himself together, out of his reverie, he got on with the business at hand.

"Good evening, Americans. We are ready to take back America, so pay close attention, as this applies to just about everybody, and those left out this evening will be a part of our next get together. You will never see me or hear from me unless I have something solid to share. Nobody wants to hear about what may or may not come in the future, so, here is what we have so far.

First of all, if you are between the ages of 20 and 50, a male in fairly good condition, report to your local police station tomorrow and get yourself hired as a cop. This will be on-the-job training. We do not have time to put you through any courses just yet. There is work to be done, and you are going to do it. Don't bother to go if you are not in good shape physically because you will be turned away, and remember what I told you about causing trouble. The police are authorized to lock you up immediately if you in any way disturb this employment effort. People are hungry and we have no time for any nonsense.

Your first jobs will be to go through the files of all known pedophiles, and if you find they have sexually assaulted a child, you will pick them up...lock them up. When your lockup is full, or you have determined that there are no more perpetrators in your area, that you are aware of, your captain will arrange for a military bus, with guards, to pick up the criminals and transport them to a compound to be castrated. Before you even ask, all you defense attorneys, they have no civil rights. From this day forward, any person who does harm to another person loses his civil rights at the second he violates those of another person. After castration, they will have the letter "C" burned into their left wrists.

The Federal Government has taken control of every police station in America and will be paying the employees. Your local governments will take some responsibilities for cost, but absolutely nobody gets laid off without my personal approval.

Your second task will be to arrest all known gang members who have been killing, looting, mugging, and maiming the citizens of your towns and cities. Once again you will lock them up to capacity, your captain will call military guards to pick them up and take them to the Nevada desert, where they will build a massive prison under the direction of skilled labor and under guard by the military. They will have to work to earn their food, tent, clothes, supplies and anything else they wish or require. They will not be paid a dime, but rather will work for points, which will be applied to their purchases at the prison store. Obviously, those who do not work do not eat or drink. One free bottle of water will be issued each morning and each evening. Everything else has to be earned. Any man who steals from another will be flogged. Any man who bullies another into giving up his possessions will reside in the jail being built, with absolutely nothing: no mail, radio, TV, gym equipment, or anything else considered comfort items. They will receive bedding, clothing, and food. That is it! None of these people will send or receive any mail or packages. Any person trying to get through the lines to see anybody will be escorted to the closest local jail and forgotten. We will worry about them three or four years from now.

You will probably find that many of the street gang members are little brothers or just little kids with no home or home life who live and steal on the streets, trying to stay alive. They are just as dangerous as the older members; all will be picked up and transported to Nevada. Parents will not be notified because they will know that if their kid disappears, he got picked up. They already know they're in gangs and believe me, they don't care. Most of the parents are addicts and will just carry on in their haze without ever missing a child who does not appear in the home every now and again. You will be keeping a roster of pedophiles and gang members shipped out. Post that list on the outside of the police department building. Do not let anybody come into the police station on either matter, as they will just waste your time. No attorney will be allowed to represent any of these people. There will be no pleas or motions of any kind accepted or allowed.

There will be medical facilities in the Nevada desert, and highly qualified desert medical doctors will be there to assess any problems that arise. There will be no women in the desert, either from gangs or in the military guard.

Next week I will talk to you about the education system, and after that we will address jobs for women. I want them to be home to get their children started in the new education system.

If you have any questions, talk to each other and discuss your concerns. We are working hard here and do not have time to adjust our thinking to the concerns of each of our Americans. We are just doing what is best for the multitudes first, and after we get a handle on these projects, we will begin to work on all the minor concerns.

Remember, do no harm to anyone. We will have no patience with you and your judgment will be swift, severe... permanent. Good night America." And with that, she got up and left the room. John just stood there taking in the moment before he decided he needed to breathe.

The entire country erupted at the same time. Everybody had something to say about everything. The best conversations were between the attorneys who just saw a great deal of money fly out the window because they could not collect for defending the scum of the earth.

Men who knew they were qualified for the job of being a policeman ran to take showers, called their buddies, just in case they had not heard, and decided to sleep on the steps of the police station to be as close to first in line as possible. Who knew how many were needed. None of them knew that the moment they were hired, they would each receive a check of $1, 000 to keep their families afloat until payday and thereby could concentrate on the jobs at hand without worry. They would never have to pay back that money. It was a gift for their courage and loyalty to help clean up America. It was a solid bet that they would share their good fortune with all family and friends who cared to listen. Roy gave Dottie a quick kiss and out the door he ran to carpool with his closest friends to the police station. He could not get the grin off of his face. He was halfway there when he realized he had never asked Dottie if she minded his being a cop. Desperation took on its own rules.

It was exactly a month later when the announcement came that Madam President would talk to the people again. She made sure that the newscasters announced the importance of having the children present this evening.

Roy was hurrying Dottie up and insisted that they eat on the couch, in front of the TV, just to be sure that they did not miss a word of what the President was about to say. Even though they had no children of their own, someday they would, and they wanted to know what was in store for the kids of America.

She entered the Oval Office with such an air, that the temperature in the entire room changed. John automatically came to a position of attention in awe of her. "All right John, here we go again," she said, and John just replied, "Yes ma'am!" He nearly fainted with pride. She knew his name. Somehow she had learned his name and cared enough to remember it and it gave him a real sense of worth to be remembered. History would never mention him, but he was *here*, making his own family history.

She settled into her chair, placed her papers in front of her, and looked to John. He was going to tell the President what to do for the second time. Does life get any more special than this? "Madam President, we go live in 5-4-3-2-GO!" And go she did!

"Good evening Americans." This evening we will first discuss the children and their education. Now children, listen to me carefully, for I am about to give you control of your futures, and you had better be careful to protect what you are about to receive. Public schools are all now under Federal control. Parents, you will place your child in the school either nearest your home or most conveniently located near your work, if you wish to take your child back and forth to school. Each child will eat breakfast and lunch at school, will be issued uniforms, and will receive whatever supplies are needed for his/her work. As parents, your job is to take care of your child, see to his/her health, happiness and good dental care. There will be no more sex education in schools; that's your job. See to it that you do your job. Any child who is being abused at home by anybody, only needs to tell the school nurse and that child will go immediately into protective custody. Abuse comes in many forms. Step-parents can mentally bruise a child by being just plain mean verbally, and that child can suffer from that abuse for the rest of his life. Be kind to your children. That is a warning. Best you heed it well. All children will have free time during the day to play, and they will be learning to play board games to stimulate their imaginations. School is to be a time of fun while learning. There will be no more bullies, and there will be no tolerance for children who have no desire to learn anything and continually disturb classes just for the joy of keeping others from learning. If your child cannot or will not learn, he will be removed from public school and placed in a trade school where he will learn a skill. He will learn to read, write, and do simple math so as not to become a bigger burden on society as an adult than he already is as a child. Some children simply cannot learn, for one reason or another, through no fault of their own. These children will have special schools to attend to teach them the life chores of taking care of their own needs, and from there they will be evaluated as to whether or not they can do any task at all that would earn them a salary as an adult. Each child is precious, and each one is going to get everything he/she desires, but will work to achieve anything and everything.

Teen pregnancies are no longer to be tolerated in public school. If your child becomes pregnant, she will be expelled and will then have to find her own way to become educated, at her own expense, in her own time.

What all children need to know, right here, right now, is that an education is no longer your right, but your privilege. If you in any way abuse the system, the teachers, or the students, out you go, and once you are out, you never return. There will be no suspensions for bad behavior. There will only be expulsions. If you do not want to learn anything, but prefer to go through life as an illiterate imbecile, that is your choice, but you will never obtain any state or federal aid simply because you have made your choice to be worthless. If you cannot succeed in public school or trade school, you are on your own, and if you commit any crime to take from others what they worked hard to gain for themselves, you will go straight to prison...and there you will remain.

School begins Monday morning. Make your decisions this weekend where you want your children to go to school, and make certain they understand the consequences of their behavior. Your lack of supervision may cost your child his future. Remember that you are the parents. Do your job!

Men and women may report to their local Unemployment Office to be hired to help build, refurbish, and work in the trade school in their area. In the cases of large cities, there will be more than one trade school. What the cities and towns need has been left up to the local school boards and the mayor's office. They have exactly one week to finalize their plans.

I bid you all good night, and look forward to talking with the women next month." She exited the room and took all the air with her as she went.

John wanted to tap dance all over the oval office. He had children, and she had just answered every prayer he had ever had about their welfare. He could not wait to get home and join in the family conversations that had surely already begun. *Heaven help us, we are going to have a super country again!*

Roy was second in line at the police station, directly behind his best friend Larry, who had three kids and an ill wife. Larry's mother was at his home taking care of everybody. If only one job was available, Roy wanted Larry to have it before anybody else.

The Captain opened the door at 3 a.m., seeing it was pointless to let the men wait. He had the door blocked so he could make sure each applicant was qualified before even letting him inside. He would ask about age, education, any medical problems that might be serious, and weight. It was obvious, by looking at the individual, if he was too fat, too sick or too old, but he wanted to give each man as much pride in himself as possible. He hired thirty men. Once he had them in the conference room, he walked around and handed out thirty checks. Each man had difficulty in holding back the tears. He made sure that they understood that the money was never to be paid back. They would receive uniforms in the afternoon. They would be paid every two weeks. That was all they needed to know just now. Forms were distributed for each man to complete, and their jobs were explained. Lunch was furnished, and uniforms were picked up. They were all told to go home, rest well, and report for duty at 7 a.m. the next day, and every day thereafter except Sunday. And off they went. Men again! Men taking care of their families, just the way they are supposed to, and keeping them safe, just the way men are supposed to, in every country in the world.

As promised, one month later the President was to speak, and this time to the women. This was going to be the hardest program to promote because women can be downright malicious to other women who do not care for children properly, but this was a program that had to be instituted, monitored carefully, and justified mentally with every woman she put to work.

"Evening John, we are both late for supper." She placed a candy bar in his hand, and John knew he would never touch a bite of it, but would wrap it in plastic and keep it as a family heirloom forever. He placed it in his handkerchief to preserve her fingerprints and gingerly placed it into his shirt pocket. She grinned to herself as she took her seat. She had seen what John did with the candy, and it pleased her immensely that he thought so much of her.

"Madam President, we go live in 5-4-3-2-GO!"

"Good evening Americans and a very special good evening to the women of America. It is now your turn to help turn this country into a place of pride and safety. It is time for many of you to go back to work. This job is for women only. You must be younger than fifty, have a college degree, and have had at least one child. Even if you had a child, but that child is now deceased, grown and no longer living in your home, the requirement is that you have had a child and understand that a child must be cared for 24/7. It is one thing to say that your duty to a child is around the clock, every day of the week, but having to perform this duty is much different from just watching others do it and walking away. If you meet the requirements given, go to your local Social Services Department tomorrow. They know how many women they need and are prepared and waiting for your arrival. You will have a caseload that is small enough that you will get to know each family extremely well and understand why they are on benefits. If you discover a home where the parent(s) are dopers or the children live in squalor, you will have the police seize the children and immediately cut off all benefits the family may be receiving. The parent(s) can live on the streets and eat from garbage cans for all I or anyone else cares, but the children deserve a fighting chance to be educated and to live a decent life. We do not want children of dopers becoming dopers and then raising dopers of their own. I'm sorry to have to say that we have thousands of women who have one child after the next, with no idea who the fathers may be, just for the sole purpose of getting free benefits so they can buy their street drugs. You are the ones who will put a stop to this. If you do not have the heart for this work, do not apply. There will be other opportunities.

Now, concerning the children you have to remove from horrible situations...hundreds of small orphanages are being built near schools, for these children, so they can walk to school. Children that you seize in your town will be moved to another town to keep them safe from the influence and continued cruelty of their parent(s). Perhaps next year we will be able to begin building rehabilitation facilities for those who wish to get off of their life-consuming addictions. We are still working on the required length of stay, but I can assure you that when the final decision is made, these people will be undergoing a life change that will hopefully continue to improve their lives long after their release. The stay in these facilities will not be a short one, as addicts have no skills, no pride, and no ability to care for themselves. They will have to learn everything about survival in order to live.

In a few weeks I will be addressing all single people about work that will be most satisfying. However, these jobs will take you away from home for at least a year and more, so begin thinking now about your future. If you are planning to accept a job away from home, you need to begin to plan where to store your belongings as you will take only bare essentials with you when you go. These jobs will be open to all singles that are in fairly decent health and are under the age of 60. You cannot have any physical disabilities, but minor mental challenges will not be a problem. If you are a single with children, you must be able to prove that the children have good care in your absence.

Good luck on your new jobs beginning tomorrow. You will be challenged as never before, but I have an enormous amount of faith in American women, and I know you will each do a good job. As always, it is a great pleasure being able to send hope your way. Good night America!"

The President looked at John, smiled, and left the room. He felt a sudden chill up his spine as he realized why she never left the White House. Somebody was waiting to kill her. It was like an announcement in his head. *She is going to die!* And he knew *why* he knew her fate. She was giving America back to the people. They were becoming involved in every aspect of life, getting in control, and they were never going to give that control back. Never again would a president be elected simply because he had money, knew the right power people, and made flowery promises that he never intended to keep. No president would ever again throw lavish parties in the White House, at the expense of the hard-working Americans. Never again would a president or a first lady run all over the world on vacations, at the expense of the hard-working man in the street, and gloat about it through TV media coverage. What a slap in the face to Americans with no jobs and no way to take care of their families. Taxes were to be used for the betterment of America, to serve Americans, not for luscious clothes and parties and vacations for those who were living in the White House. After this woman, anybody who ran for office had better have a good plan for running the country and keeping everybody working and safe, especially the children, or the public would simply tear them from office, one way or another. This position was no longer a joke; it was a serious business, and this was a serious President. She was surely going to have many enemies, and they would be vicious and cruel, doing anything and everything to silence her voice. She knew this…John knew she knew this. He prayed for her every day and hoped she would accomplish a great deal before she was eliminated. He hoped she would serve her entire ten years and never leave the White House because the nation needed a president who could make a decision without worrying about whether she had everybody's approval rating. She did what was right and she was setting the standard, a very high standard, for those who would follow her Presidency.

It was six weeks before John saw the President again. All his single friends had been hounding him to let them know what she had in mind. They all wanted to work. They knew it would be something grand, and they were all packed and ready to go, but John knew absolutely nothing and continued to tell them so, even though they did not believe him. Finally, the night arrived, and he was as anxious as anybody to learn what the new project was to be…and then here she came to tell America.

"Evening John, it's another wonderful evening."

"Yes Ma'am."

She sat down, sighed, grinned his way, and was ready.

"Madam President, we go live in 5-4-3-2-GO!"

"Good evening Americans. We are about to lay some foundations to help feed America. All you singles who have been anxiously awaiting this news, I hope you will be pleased. If you do not know where a National Park is located nearest to you, look it up on the Internet, or call the number you see on your screen and find out. We are going into the parks to plant fruit and nut trees, grape vines, anything at all that will grow and furnish food, entirely on its own, year after year. This food will be there, free for the taking, and there will be Forest Rangers on staff to make sure that nobody is taking more than he/she needs for his/her family, for the sole purpose of selling it to others. This food is not to be sold. It is to be enjoyed by all who come to the park. When food is available, vehicles will be searched coming and going through the park gates. Offenders will be fined and forbidden to ever return to any park in the US. Now, getting yourself to a park may be a problem. If so, the same location number will arrange for you to be picked up and taken to a park to work. Some of these sites have hundreds of miles of land, and a great deal of it will be planted. When you arrive, you will be given a backpack with the basic necessities to survive in the wild. The leaders will be knowledgeable about the vegetation in their prospective areas. Not every fruit or vegetable will grow in every area. You will have a great deal of information to carry back to your own family and friends when your work is finished. Growing food and teaching others how to grow food will be a very satisfying vocation indeed.

I would also like to encourage all the places of worship in America to take a look at their grounds and determine if they could plant fruit or nut trees, grape vines, anything edible. Plant anything and everything that is perennial and let the people enjoy fresh foods. There is joy in the planting, joy in the caring for the plants and trees while they grow, and lots of joy in the eating. Don't let any opportunity to grow food go to waste.

It has been a pleasure helping you get started in cleaning up America. You will not see me for several months as I need to evaluate how all the programs are progressing, pull out the weeds that are choking the programs, and see where we will be headed next. Good luck to each of you."

She gathered up her papers and off she went, once again leaving an ecstatic John to evaluate what he just heard. *The woman wants us to plant food so we can all eat. Why is it that nobody ever thought of that before?*

Keith was dressed and ready to go to the meeting, with the President, at the White House. The assignment was right up his alley. He was a Green Beret, with twenty years of service under his belt, and had been in situations far more demanding than this. This time, it would be a matter of keeping the President alive. Her idea was brilliant, and he knew he could pull it off. He spoke several languages quite fluently and had infiltrated a great many organizations, never to be discovered. Today, he would find out if his own American buddies in fighting crime were good enough to cast him out as an imposter.

The meeting was to start at 11:00 a.m.; a few seconds before, the President walked in and asked her right-hand-man Geoffrey to lock the doors. It was a strange thing to do in the White House. Her purpose was to lock out anybody who was late. She herself had taped a note on the outside of the door that read, YOU ARE LATE, GO AWAY!

Everybody rose as she went to the front of the room. She asked them to be seated and then began the shock treatment.

"There are a lot of Secret Service men in this room. Do you all know each other?" The answers were just mumbles as they looked around at one another. They were brothers-in-arms and did not really know each other well, but felt that they could recognize one another from previous assignments. She asked again. "Do you each know every other man in this room?" This time they began to look around diligently, but still nobody made any comment. She pointed to one man and asked him to get up and tell her the names of every man in the third row. Naturally, he could not do it, and managed only about half of them, several of which were mispronounced.

Grinning, she said, "Gentlemen, you will notice that in the back of the room are sandwiches, fruit, cookies, and water. While you are walking around with your finger foods, you will please find the impersonators who are here to kill me. Fortunately for me, this is a test. And hopefully, when I return, in one hour, you will have them handcuffed and in the front of the room under guard."

And with that, she went to the door, Geoffrey unlocked it, they exited, and Geoffrey relocked it, pulled up a chair, and sat guard. Off she went for her own lunch just about to chuckle out loud. *Let's see just how good that Green Beret actually is with American Secret Service. My money is on my own men.*

Her money would have been ill placed. When she returned and approached the door, Geoffrey told her that there had just been conversation and a bit of laughter until about quarter of twelve. At that point, things got heated, some of the men were shouting, and it sounded as if a bit of shoving was going on every few minutes. She just grinned, and he opened the door for her. As she entered, she knew her bet was a lousy one, as there were two Secret Service men in the front of the room wearing handcuffs. She addressed them both by name, apologized that their peers did not know them, had their cuffs removed, and asked everybody to please sit down. Red faces were all around the room...except one, who was wearing a slight grin and munching on a cookie.

"The purpose of this exercise was to let you know that an imposter can break through the ranks at any time. An imposter in this room would be here for only one reason, and that is to kill the President. According to the exercise, I am already dead. Keith, would you please come up here and introduce yourself."

Keith rose from his chair, went to the front of the room, and rather than tell them who he was, said, "I am very very good at what I do. I can, and have, infiltrated many places, for the sole purpose of killing somebody, and I have never, ever failed. The world is full of men and women just like me, and if one of them had been here today, your President would be dead right now. You absolutely must know each other by face and name, and anytime you feel, even just *barely* feel that something is not right, grab that person and cuff him. You can always apologize later, but you cannot apologize if your Commander-In-Chief is killed on your watch."

"But who *are* you," someone yelled out.

"Your worst nightmare, if you ever let this happen again!" And with that, he bowed to the President and out he went before anybody could really put his facial features into their memory banks. He lived because he was a blur to everybody, and he meant to keep it that way.

"Geoffrey, pass out the cards, and the meeting will be adjourned."

The cards were very small, like tiny kiddie cards. She had stolen the idea from when cards were handed out to soldiers during wartime so they could recognize the leaders of the enemy. It worked so well, that she figured it would work well for the agents to learn the names and faces of one another. Down the road there would be another test; but they would never be prepared for it, and would have to react in split seconds.

Members of the Congress and members of the Senate were to hear reports and see documentaries on the ongoing projects. Afterwards they could discuss if these were worthwhile, based solely on results. Every report and every film would show the good and the bad. She would not allow them to vote on any of the projects before they went into effect as they would be arguing over insignificant details while the people were starving and streets were getting more dangerous. Well, the streets were still dangerous, but just not *as* dangerous, and she had great plans for murderers, especially parents who murdered their children. She had wanted to attend at least one of these showings, but after the agent fiasco she did not feel safe, even in the White House. She could not die; she had a great deal to do for the people. And why the hell weren't there any women in the Secret Service? She decided to find out that very afternoon.

Not liking large meetings, as nothing ever got done, she called in three people who could advise her regarding why no women were on the Secret Service Staff. What she heard made her want to kick some prejudicial ass. As she rose, she told them that within a month she wanted to see at least six women, in her office, who could beat the hell out of a Green Beret. She did not care what they looked like; they could be amazons, or four-foot tigers, but as long as they were fearless, she wanted to see them.

The second she closed the door the moaning and groaning began. Oh, they all knew that she would be infiltrating women everywhere. Why couldn't they just do their little lady-like jobs and stay the hell out of men's business. Put a woman in the mix and right away you have mad wives, jealous girlfriends and all kinds of shenanigans going on to distract the men, who would be the only ones really doing the job anyway!

In three weeks, as required of them, there were half a dozen women in her office, and each had an attitude and an air about her that immediately incited fear. "All right, ladies, follow me."

They went to the gymnasium, in the White House, and guess who was there, at her invitation again? There stood Keith, ready and willing to put each and every butt straight up in the air and straight down again, knocking the wind out of them, in order to end the qualification test quickly. The first three were quick and easy, but then, number four approached. She let out her breath and waited for him to attack. The other three had attacked him, and that was a big mistake. He had the height, weight, and power. To get him, one had to grab him on the run, get him off balance, and lay him out with a knife at his throat. And that is what she did. He was so stunned that he just lay there looking into her eyes and said the dumbest thing that came to mind. "I sure hope you're not married." Everybody laughed, thinking that he meant she would be a dangerous wife, but what he actually meant was that he had every intention of marrying this wild woman himself. He had waited all his life, for the right woman, and he knew he would know her the very second they touched. And touch they did. His butt hurt, she had a knife at his throat, and her eyes were blazing. Oh, he was in love all right.

The next two ladies were just about as bad as the first three, and she thanked them all for coming, asked Geoffrey to give them their inconvenience checks, thanked Keith, and got the woman's name while he was still listening. She did not have the heart to cheat him out of that. Her name was Melody Cross. That was just about as dumb a name as he had ever heard, and he was pretty sure that she had made it up and had some name change in her past. *Melody* sounds like a sweet southern girl, but cross her at your peril. His heart was pumping his brains out and he got out, as fast as he could.

"Melody, my dear, here is the offer. Do you want to be a Secret Service Agent and if so, would you mind occupying one of the rooms here in the White House?" Melody simply agreed and did not even ask what the salary would be…and Maude did not miss that deletion. She wasn't just a tough old broad, she was extremely suspicious and alert to everything said and how it was said. "And Melody, you will be my own personal protector. If I go down, chances are you will go with me, or instead of me. Can you live with that?"

"That is who I am, and that is what I do. But you will never go down with me by your side, and that is a solemn promise." Now the President felt that she had what she had needed all along. She had never really felt safe, and had always been looking over her shoulder or behind her. Now she could just concentrate on the business at hand and *Melody* could be looking over her shoulder and behind her. Things were certainly looking up! But still and all, some checking needed to be done before she would be completely at ease with this strange woman. Why had the woman come if she did not care about the salary? Little details like that bothered her, and she would not be content until she knew everything there was to know about the woman in whose hands she was placing her life.

The next day Keith was in her office and his face was blood red. That was a never-before experience for him and quite humiliating.

"Now Keith, I know you were quite taken with Melody. And you did something, or actually, did *not* do something that I found to be quite disturbing. She had a bottle of water, which she left sitting in a corner when she came up to strip you of your masculinity. You failed to take the bottle with you when you left. I know because I watched the tape back and saw quite clearly that you were taken by this woman. I began to wonder if it had been anybody else, if you would have grabbed that bottle and had the fingerprints traced just looking for some dent in that massive armor she wears. So?"

Keith had been caught by the one woman in the world he respected, even more than some of his fearless buddies. He wanted her protected more than anything else in his life, and knew he would be the one to exact revenge if anybody ever so much as touched a hair on her head. All he could do was grin. "I'm willing to bet that my folks will do the normal background check and she will come up clean. But I'm also willing to bet that if *you* do another thorough check, the kind you know how to do very well, you are going to find something that is not exactly right. She was perfect for the two jobs: one of getting hired, and the other of turning your head so that you lost your sense of suspicion. What do you think?"

All of a sudden Keith felt the bell ring in his head, and he was only too aware that he may have been a victim of this striking and self-sufficient woman. He felt wounded. "I will search every nook and cranny of this woman's life and dig out any dirt I can. But I am also doing it thoroughly to prove to my very favorite woman, in the world, that she is safe with her private guard."

Maude made sure that the documentaries being shown to the members of the Congress and Senate were supremely confidential. No news media people and absolutely no family or guests would be invited. Great precautions were taken to make certain that the precious films were kept secret. She wanted everybody to have an opportunity to discuss the pros and cons of each project without the infiltration of the media input trying to make good stories out of every detail. The viewing went quite well; some questions were asked and answered, and it seemed that it might be time to get on with the business at hand, and let those in charge of the on-going projects continue to do what they were doing so well.

She had two big moves left. She decided to institute the one that would bring immediate peace to many people and let the other wait a few weeks, as it would be the one that numbered her days.

Her telecast was set for 9 p.m. because she felt it was not a subject for children and did not want parents to have to explain horrid details to their little ones. Some parents would decide to have their children listen, but that was their choice.

"Evening ma'am."

"Evening John."

John knew somebody was in for it this time, and it was not going to be pleasant. He readied himself as she sat down.

"Madam President, we are live in 5-4-3-2-GO."

"Good evening Americans. Once again we must talk. This is not a pleasant subject, and the matter is going to be explosive, but this country has been allowing people to murder children for too many years, and the murderers have figured out ways to go free without punishment. Our lopsided system has required prosecutors to convince a jury, beyond a shadow of a doubt, by proving without question, that an individual, frequently a parent, killed a child. That stops now, this evening, this minute. Any person suspected of killing a child under the age of 18 will immediately be given a truth serum, and if he/she admits to killing the child and describes the killing in such detail that there is no question as to guilt, he/she will be euthanized immediately. His/her body and all the belongings that were on that person will be cremated directly afterward, and flushed. Nothing will be given to the family of this murderer and there will be no place for them to go to mourn.

Presently, across the country, we have dozens of people suspected of murdering children. Some are in jail awaiting trial; some are not. They will be given a truth serum and questioned immediately. For the innocent people, this will be a blessing for them as they can prove that they are innocent and the police can then concentrate their efforts elsewhere. The entire confession of each murderer will be available for your review at any time. Parents who insist their precious sons and daughters are innocent of any crime can listen to their child describe his/her monstrous behavior, and malicious intent. We are going to make every effort to put an end to the murder of children. It is your job to help the police when you have information that may help them solve a case. For those of you who have lost children, and nobody has paid the price, be patient a little longer, and hopefully we will be able to ease your pain. We may find the bodies of many of our lost children so we can put them to rest. Good night Americans. Sleep well as we are working hard to make your lives first bearable... and then happy and comfortable. We have one more project coming, and then it will be time to hear from those of you who have wonderful ideas about how to improve the economy, save on energy, and how to keep our own citizens fully employed."

With that she rose and left the room, looking haggard and worried. She was not as light-hearted as normal. John attributed her appearance to the kind of message she had to give to America this evening. It was a horrible thing to think of the man or woman who knew that he/she had killed a child, would admit to that crime under the truth serum, and once having done that, would be killed like an animal being euthanized, burnt to a crisp and flushed, ending up a nobody because there would be no grave marker. He/she would just be gone from the world. Killers everywhere were screaming for attorneys, but they were to find that attorneys simply turned them in for the rewards. They had been cheated out of a great many cases, and the government had placated them by rewarding them to turn in killers that they could not represent anyway. It was just a matter of one hand washing the other. There was to be no consideration regarding mental illness, background of abuse or any other excuse. Once a child was killed, one had to assume that this individual would kill again and had to be stopped in the most permanent ways available.

Maude was so tired her bones ached. She had known for a long time that the old ticker could not take the pace at which she worked, but she was adamant with the old heart strings that she intended to get this job at least started in the right direction for the people, even if she did not last to see it through. She did not have to worry about being popular or loved or even whether or not she could win reelection, because she would not be around for any of it to matter. The VP, John White, was a close and trusted friend, and she knew that he would carry on the work she had started as well as develop some of his own ideas for the future of the country. He wanted to see workers in factories and mills again, producing products that now came from overseas. He wanted everything sold in America to say that it was made by an American. Maude had met John in college, and they had gone to rallies together, protests for better conditions wherever needed, and agreed on just about every issue. The ones on which they disagreed called for discussions into the wee hours of the night. He had been like a brother to her and she a sister to him. Neither had any parents left, so Maude took the role of grandmother to his children and they adored her. He was the one who convinced her to run for office. He told her that only she had the nerve to begin the programs, but he would have the dedication to see that her efforts were continued after her death. Neither could have had a better friend.

Geoffrey had never entered the President's bedroom before and was truly skeptical about his poor choice to do so now, but he just had to talk with her about her new project, because she had overlooked something truly important and he could not finish the report without her input. After giving it long consideration, he rang her room and asked if she felt it an impropriety to bring her the report to review so he could finish before morning. Maude had no qualms about Geoffrey coming to her bedroom. Good grief, the boy was like a son to her, and she adored and trusted him completely; she had even included him in her will.

Keith sat quite still as he read and reread the information about Melody. She had a spotless background, with her Master's Degree coming shortly on the heels of her Bachelor's, both majors in Criminal Justice. Her employment with the FBI immediately followed graduation. Her picture really did not do her justice. It was something about the eyes; they were too soft, too genuine. They were not the eyes poised over his, blazing with fury. The day before she interviewed for the job with Secret Service, she took a six-month leave of absence, noting family problems as the reason. And that is what made no sense whatever. Why not just tell the FBI that you were going to do an interview at the White House? If you did not get the job, you would still be a hit in the office because you were invited in the first place. Or, why not just take the day off and not tell anybody anything? Keith could not wrap his mind around this confusing detail. He decided that he would either have to go to her parents' home and inquire about this so-called family problem or go mad trying to figure it out. He was used to everything being above board, easy to understand. He knew who was good and who was bad and never had to worry about a good man *maybe* being bad. None of this made any sense to him. The parents lived about fifteen minutes from his hotel, so he decided to just drop in on them without warning and thereby get a better picture of who might be hiding something. It took a few minutes less than he had gauged as the traffic was light and the home was easy to find. He rang the doorbell and had his first words ready on his lips when Melody answered the door.

"What are *you* doing here?"

"I live here. And just who might you be?"

"You know exactly who I am. You threw me on my ass in the White House gym and crammed a knife under my throat, so the least you can do is remember me."

"Oh, my God. You met somebody that called herself Melody, and you think that it's me. She grabbed him by the front of his shirt, yanked him in the house and slammed the door. *My* name is Melody Cross, and you met my twin, who sometimes uses my background as her own. Just tell me, please, that she is not in the White House, because if she is, she is there to kill the President. The family disowned her years ago when we discovered that she is a gun for hire, usually by drug cartels. I know I'm talking fast, but whoever you are, if you can call the White House and have her arrested, you may just save the President." And with that Keith was on the phone, directly into the phone of a Secret Service Agent on the floor of the President's living quarters.

Geoffrey had been in her room for a few minutes discussing what he found lacking in the proposed program. A wall was going to be built miles and miles wide, and twenty feet high with lookouts. It was going to keep Mexico out and America in and absolutely no trucks would ever be allowed to enter America through the only two checkpoints. Every single car would be inspected and sniffed by dogs, and a picture would be taken of the people in the car, along with their fingerprints. She intended to put such a dent in the Mexican drug cartels trafficking that they would have to look elsewhere for customers. She would also put hundreds of people to work. She needed to say who could be employed, and she needed to make the decision to say whether or not she would allow any Mexicans to work on the wall, or be employed to guard the wall and the checkpoints. She decided they could not be employed in any capacity. It was best for them and she would explain; if they still had relatives in Mexico, they could be intimidated to help the cartels or their relatives would be killed.

Maude was sitting up in the bed reading and making notes when she realized she needed her heart medication. She asked Geoffrey to go into the bathroom, and bring her the green bottle and a bottle of the spring water. He entered the bathroom, opened the cabinet to retrieve her water and pills, and noticed her gun lying beside the pill bottle. He heard the door to her bedroom open and close very softly. He automatically picked up the gun but kept himself hidden and quiet.

"Melody dear, do you need something?" There was nothing but a stifled scream as Melody yanked the pillow from beneath her head and crammed it over her face. At that moment the door crashed open and somebody shot her in the back just as Geoffrey lunged from the bathroom and shot her in the right temple. The force of the firepower into her body flung her off the bed with the pillow still in her hands. Geoffrey jumped on the bed, dropped the gun beside the President, and scooped her up into his arms, crying and screaming for her to say she was okay.

"My heart," was all she could utter. Geoffrey ran to the bathroom for the forgotten pills, grabbed a bottle of water, again cradled her in his arms, and fed her the medicine. Maude had automatically slipped the gun into the pocket of her robe. She felt safe with the gun touching her hip. She liked guns and she knew how to use them. She had no less than eight guns scattered around her bedroom.

An automatic relay of emergency calls had gone out the second Keith's call was received, and everybody was running *for* the White House and those inside were running toward the President's bedroom. The ambulance had already arrived, and the medic and a doctor were running down the hallway with a gurney. Melody's body was on the floor right beside the bed, preventing the medic from getting the gurney next to the bed. The Secret Service men dragged Melody from the room and shoved her against the wall in the hallway, thinking her dead.

They had to wrench a crying and pathetic Geoffrey off of the President who was then placed on the gurney, taken out of the White House and loaded into the ambulance. Off they went at top speed. The doctor said he had called her private physician to meet them at the hospital and then said he would make her comfortable by giving her a shot to relax her.

"It won't interfere with your heart medication; it will simply put you to sleep without any pain whatsoever. We don't want you getting too upset over this horrible incident."

"I don't know you, so how do you know my doctor's name and about my heart condition? It has been a guarded secret for several years."

"Well now, aren't we just the clever little lady?"

She knew immediately that he was Melody's backup and that her instinct to bring the gun that Geoffrey had dropped next to her paid off. She shot him through the heart. He was still holding the poisoned needle when he went down. The driver slammed on the brakes, jumped out, and ran, with Secret Service men chasing him down and not knowing why. Two of them snatched open the back of the ambulance, guns pointed at a dead man.

"Have that syringe tested, and you will find I was just about dead for the second time tonight. You boys are going to get me killed yet. So far I've only been saved by my secretary and myself. Why are you all on my payroll? Let's see if you can get me back to the White House in one piece. And no, before you ask, I'm not going to the hospital. Somebody is probably waiting there to kill me as well."

Back at the White House, Keith had arrived, been briefed, saw the looks on the medics' faces when they asked where the President was, and informed everybody that there was no such other ambulance sent for her. Pandemonium began immediately and got worse when Keith inspected Melody and discovered that she wore a protective vest that caught and stopped the bullet in her back. Her only injury was Geoffrey's shot to her temple. He instructed the medics to take her to the hospital, and he and one of the Secret Service men went with them. The President called him back to the White House the next day to explain everything that had happened and to assure him that his timing was impeccable, as always. He asked permission to give her a hug, which she granted, and said that was all the reward he would ever need, and since he could never top his latest heroics, it was time for him to return to his unit. He did, however, request permission to stay in touch, just in case a juicy job came up in the future, and they not only hugged, but laughed as well.

Unfortunately, for Melody, who was actually *Sarah*, it was determined that she was to live, but not to really be alive. She was brain dead and the family decided that if there was any justice, she would remain that way for one year. Then she was to have her plug pulled, be cremated, and as the President had said, be FLUSHED!

Nobody has ever been able to prove one way or the other whether the so-called brain dead is aware of anything. Can they hear with their subconscious? Are they aware of their horrible circumstances? The family hoped that Sarah could both hear and was aware that in one year she was to be harvested for any vital organs of use to others, then cremated and flushed. There had to be some kind of justice in this world, and this felt very much like justice. Nobody would ever know if Sarah knew anything, but everybody hoped that she did.

Madam President lasted one more year until her heart condition was so bad that she could not continue, but during her time in office she put thousands and thousands of people back to work. She had finished the rehabilitation centers, and all offenders arrested for driving while on dope, committing burglaries while drugged up, or attacking someone, found themselves in one of the centers for two years minimum. There was no release at all until they proved themselves free of drugs, able to perform some kind of job, and willing to relocate away from the people and places that had sent them into the drug hell in which they had lived.

John moved up from Vice President to President and made Maude proud as he implemented his own programs for the betterment of America and continued the ones she had put in force. It was a new America. Children understood the need for a good education, the troubled students had trade schools to give them purpose, there was some control over drugs, and everybody had an opportunity to work. Crime decreased so much that over-crowding was no longer a problem in the prison system.

There would never be another Maude Rugsby, but every President thereafter would try to be a hard-working, truthful President. Naturally there would be bad Presidents to cite as the worst leaders ever, but now they had Maude to emulate.

Geoffrey remained at the White House as a trusted and faithful secretary to each president he served until he retired, and with the money Maude left him, bought a little business on the beach. Rather than let any profits go to waste, he helped to support many of the projects that Maude began, and left everything to a trade school when he died.

Keith made a couple of visits to the Cross home and got to know more about the real Melody, but she never made the impression on him that he could remember so well from his experience in the gym. He finally decided that he was not going to find a mate in this life because the kind of woman who excited his mind right into marriage was apparently always going to be bad. When he was 65 he would discover he was wrong, but that is another story...

ANIMAL INSTINCT

Tomorrow would be Victor's birthday, but he knew there would be no celebration, of any kind, by anybody. He had a home for one more night, and then he was on his own. Much to his family's surprise, he had graduated from high school, but they did not attend. He was not sad or unhappy; in fact, he was so relieved that he was almost unable to control his delight. He decided to wait until everyone was in bed and then slip into the kitchen for something to eat, grab his coat and his well-packed backpack, and leave his home through the backdoor…forever.

Victor remembered the hard years when he had to pretend to be on drugs, to be stealing alcohol, not doing his schoolwork and deliberately making bad grades. All of those character flaws fell right about the times when he would vanish for several days. When he returned, he would listen to the lectures and endure the punishments and then just up and act like an idiot again when it was necessary. His parents never had any illusions about him going to college or joining the military or doing anything of consequence, and after eighteen years, they told him that the day he turned of age, they wanted him out of their home. They had two other perfectly normal children, who worked hard in school and would build good futures for themselves. They never had any idea that Victor was not their child, but *he* knew, and he had known since he was fifteen years old.

He knew from an early age that there was something wrong with him, something creepy and different, but it scared him so badly that he could not tell anybody how he felt, and, anyway, he did not know what he felt but he knew it was somehow awful. People would just think him nuts if he said he thought he was different from everybody else. He knew he could not explain how he felt, so he just kept silent.

On the day he turned fifteen years old, he finally found out what was wrong with him and that it was time for him to begin acting like a loser so the family would easily turn him loose without a hitch. He could not go to any rehab centers, or AA for kids, as all these places would do blood tests and his was beginning to turn and he could not be found out, but must stay secret in every way. The man explained to him that he was a government experiment and a very expensive one, and that they would be watching his every move, every day until he turned eighteen. He would do as he was told or they would simply pick him up and his parents would think he had either run away or had been kidnapped, but that would put the parents through a lot of trauma for no reason.

However, they would not really care very much about his disappearance after the nightmares he was about to put them through. It would be much kinder for him to just follow their instructions and spare his parents more grief than was necessary. Victor was told that he could perform on his own, or someone would be there to put the drugs in his system, the alcohol down his throat, and to keep him locked up for several days before turning him loose looking like he had been sleeping in a gutter. Even though it was a shock for him to hear that he was an experiment, he was almost relieved because he had always known that he was nothing like his siblings. He never had the compassion for his parents that they had, never enjoyed family outings and never had any friends.

The agent told him all he could legally divulge. He explained that the boy he replaced had died in birth and he was substituted. It had been a C-section, so nobody in the family knew the baby was dead, and they were all happy when they saw him and none of the family ever realized he was not theirs. Victor had no mother at all. He was a test tube baby, developed to be a specialized kind of government agent. He would learn when he was eighteen years old everything he would need to know about who...and *what...* he was. For now, from fifteen to eighteen, he needed to concentrate on becoming a nightmare for his entire family so they would let him go without any heartache. The agent told him they could not afford to have his family search for him, in any way, and all records concerning his existence were going to be destroyed when he turned eighteen. He would no longer exist.

Tomorrow was his big day, and he felt that after all these years of pretending he was something that he was not, it was only fair that he begin his new life at the stroke of midnight. He could not wait to meet the agent again and hear all about himself and how unique he must be for all the time and expense that must have gone into creating him. He could not help but imagine himself as some exceptional 007, saving the world. Unfortunately, people were still up at midnight, and he had to wait until almost 3 am before he could creep out of his old life and walk into his new future.

He had only walked two blocks when a vehicle pulled up beside him, rolled down the window and called him by name. "Ready to begin, Victor?"

And so it began. They took him to a secure compound where they gave him a very nice room with a bedroom, exercise equipment, and very strange food. There was a refrigerator full of meats, but no actual kitchen or any way to cook anything. Mr. Daniels came in to welcome him and told him that the next few days would be hard for him as his body would begin needing a different kind of food, all of which was supplied, and that his body would feel as though it was overheating sometimes, but the cooling fans would help. Everything he needed was supplied. And then he was gone. Victor never got a chance to ask how he was supposed to cook, but figured they would let him know later.

Victor was tired, and happy, and lonely, and thrilled, and all the other emotions that grate against one another when one is facing a new experience, scared out of his mind, but delighted to be on his own. He was not prepared for the burning blood churning inside his body, nor the thirst that could not be quenched or the need for raw meat that came on him in the night. He was repulsed by himself, and yet he craved everything that revolted him.

As promised, in a week, Mr. Daniels returned to his room, but he entered with several men holding guns.

"Am I dangerous"?

"Yes, indeed you are dangerous Victor. Not as much right now as you will be, but you are very dangerous. I am going to tell you what you are, and it is your reaction that worries me, because I've been through this stage with others who went completely berserk...and some we just had to put down."

"Put down? I'm not an animal that you put down; I'm a man."

"No Victor, you most certainly are *not* a man. You are actually an animal, a wild animal with a human brain and a human body, but you are a wild animal. Your appearance will begin to change as you age, and you will appear to be more of an ape than man in a few years. However, though you will lose your ability to speak, as long as we continually communicate with you, and you hear illuminating conversations between others, you will retain your ability to think and rationalize. We created you because you are going to have the strength of a monster, the will to kill anything living--in order to eat, and the ability and strength to carry out your orders. In another month, you will begin carrying out your assignments, and we will no longer feed you. If you want to eat, you will have to eat the victims you are assigned to assassinate. Your brain is wired with the ability to understand orders and follow those orders precisely. You are the most perfect killing machine in the world. We have only had to put down two of our experiments, and one female escaped. Corrections have been made to those errors, so we do not anticipate any foul-ups from here on with our assassins."

They left the room quickly before Victor sprang towards them, screaming at the top of his lungs. He wasn't dangerous yet, but in a month, he would be at the beginnings of his true development. He would begin to change in appearance, and every day he would become angrier and completely incensed with rage at his condition and that is what they needed in order for him to survive each assignment. Once he was ready for his first assassination he would be put to sleep, given his orders while unconscious, and awakened very slowly, by remote control, in the area where his target lived. He was the perfect lethal weapon. Eventually, he would lose his ability to speak, just like any animal, but he would always retain his understanding, his comprehension of how to carry out every detail for a successful mission. For him, the prey would be his meal. He was a killing machine, on the hunt whenever they needed him to be until somebody killed him. After the first three failures they had bred a dozen very efficient killers, and even though they were in the early stages of their development, in five years they would be able to turn them loose in a given area, and they would kill more people in power than a trained army, not because they were better, but because they were animals and could go where animals could go…sniff out their prey and sneak in for the kill. They were each the perfect weapon. For now they would be sent in to kill just one primary target, make their way back to the plane, and be put back to sleep until they returned to the compound. This procedure would be repeated from one assignment to the next until they were ready for release. They would not be fed for two days prior to their task to ensure they showed no mercy getting at their meal. There would come a day when they would just be turned loose in a country and left there to kill everything in a uniform. With a camera attached to their chests, the agents could just sit back and watch the war taking place, count the casualties and never lose a soldier of their own. What a remarkable way to fight a war!

Mr. Daniels stood outside Victor's room and listened to him wail for a few minutes, then slowly pushed the remote button that controlled his brain and heard him hit the floor. He looked through the peephole to be sure that there was no slipup, and then opened the door. The guards went in, put him on the stretcher, and wheeled him out to the waiting airplane. Their flight destination was secret until the plane was in the air and then only the pilot was informed. Mr. Daniels programmed Victor's brain with the information he would need to find his quarry and kill him. He was told he was free to kill anybody who got in his way, but he absolutely had to kill his target. Everybody on the plane had worked diligently on this weapons program, for years, and they took a moment to open a bottle of champagne and toast one another on their achievements.

"I am a happy man today. When we brought Francine here to kill this target we did not have the assistance of the remote button. Otherwise, when she tried to escape, I could have pressed the button and dropped her where she hid. We would have found her and then tried to discover what was wrong with her and why she did not respond to the program guidelines. Although, Mr. Kramer may have been right in saying that men enjoy a hunt and kill just by their very nature, while women have some genetics in their system that promotes mothering and prevents murdering. Right or wrong, we are not going to waste our time on women unless we are out to kill them." Everybody laughed good-heartedly and Jonathan asked if he could put his wife on that list, which caused more laughter.

Weather, it seems, never cooperates when one is looking for a smooth ride. There was a lot of turbulence as the pilot descended toward the small strip. The plane landed with such a gut-wrenching jolt that a technician was thrown against Mr. Daniels, who accidently hit the button on the remote to awaken Victor. He awoke immediately, confused and in a foggy daze, and thinking these people were challenging his mission, killed everybody on the plane, and then with a terrifying scream of power, he jumped from the plane and its dead and ran into the jungle. In his head was the map for him to follow to find the one he was to kill, but the picture was strange. He could not see the face of the man he was supposed to assassinate. All he could see was the face of a woman. He kept going along the path in his brain until he came to a river he recognized as the one he would cross just before getting to the palace. He swam across the river and sat on the bank trying to get a picture of the man he was assigned to kill. He *had* to kill. He *had* to eat. Kill the man and eat the man. That was in his brain, but there was no man to kill, only a woman. He could not make sense of the problem, and there was no way to find out anything. All he had to rely on was himself. He had nothing and nobody else.

Then he saw her, the woman in his brain. In one hand was a whip and in the other was a small child. She threw the child to the ground and snapped the whip and the scream that came from the little boy was raw enough to tear out the heart of any animal. She threw back her head and laughed. He was up and at her and killed her instantly, then began to eat her as the boy ran screaming towards the palace and his mother. Victor carried the rest of his meal into the jungle and ate slowly.

When he had finished eating he began to think about his situation. He was now completely alone. There would be nobody to tell him what to do next, to talk to him to stimulate his brain. There would be no conversations to listen to when he could no longer speak. He would never be able to explain to anybody that he was a man in his mind, but not his body. The only real thing that he knew and understood clearly was that he had to kill bad people. He could watch people from the forest and if he saw something bad, like the woman whipping the little boy, he would kill that person. He could lead a life of doing good deeds for others and that would still make him a man.

Every day he had to review everything he knew. He remembered his name. He was Victor, an animal man. His brain took him home, then to Mr. Daniels, and then he recalled the order to kill anybody that got in his way. Upon waking so quickly, he had thought everybody was in his way, and he had killed them all. Now he had nobody to put him to sleep and take him home. He was here forever. He was an animal and people would come hunting him and kill him for killing to eat. What was he to do? Did he have to live in a jungle for the rest of his life with the rest of the animals like a beast? For an instant he wanted to go home. Then he wanted Mr. Daniels. He could not stand the thought of being lost and alone.

The local natives would sit around their campfires at night and tell the story of the big ape that looks a little like a man and walks upright. If there is a man doing evil to others, the ape man will appear and carry him off, never to be seen again. He stays to himself unless some wrong is being done, and then his justice is swift and horrible. All the little native girls and boys were told that they did not have to be afraid of him as long as they were good, and were respectful to their parents.

Victor sits alone in the jungle with the few thoughts he has left. He knows to hurt the bad men, but he has little rational thought left, and no memory of his home, his parents, or Mr. Daniels and his experiment. He has nobody to talk to, nobody to stimulate his vanishing man brain, and it begins to decay. The animal instincts become more prominent every day, and soon he will no longer be any part human. He will have no understanding of right or wrong, no compassion, and no reason to punish the wicked. He will simply be an animal and he will kill and eat anything or anybody that comes along when he is hungry, regardless of its size.

Francine, by now, is pure animal and from the jungle, she has seen this animal. The law of animal instinct dictates that species must reproduce with their own kind. She has never seen one of her own kind, but is afraid to approach this male ape. He might attack and kill her as she has seen him do to so many other animals. She has no ability to think about these things, but something has kept her away from Victor. Animals learn what is right and wrong from their parents and she has had no informative animal childhood. She is without the ability to make any decisions concerning Victor.

Whether true or false, there is a native who tells his story of survival from the ape man. He explains how he was being chased by the ape man, when out of the forest came another ape, but it was a female, and they actually ran into each other.

He had no idea what happened because he continued running as fast as he could all the way to the village.

It would be nice to know that these two lost animals found some comfort in each other, but we will never know, as they were never seen again.

PRECIOUS ME

Gramma makes me so damn mad sometimes. She is making me write this story myself, about myself. Nobody can write a story about their own self without making out that they are so great and all their problems are somebody else's fault. Gramma! Now there's a woman who is capable of making a perfectly healthy dog's hair stand straight up, fall out and lose a few dog years, but we'll get to that later. Right now I need to try and describe myself without letting too much of my vanity show. I mean I know I'm extremely cute, but I have to admit that I am 6 pounds of constant fury, with a growl box that starts automatically at the slightest irritation. Damn near everything irritates me.

When I was born, I was so tiny that I fit right in the palm of the lady who came to get me and take me away from my siblings and my doggie mom who was warm and snuggly. It was not a very happy moment in my life. However, after a few days with my new Mom, I realized what an easy life I was going to have, and settled right into being spoiled.

I'm part Chihuahua and part Yorkie, jet black, with long legs, and a tendency to bark at anything that moves, including people I don't know, and sometimes people I do know. My job is to protect Mom. I am always on the alert for rabid squirrels, diving birds, and leaves that float through the air and could easily put out a Mom's eye. In fact, I've been known to bark continually for hours. Mom has tried all the gadgets to get me to stop barking so much, but it is just ingrained, and I will protect her in spite of herself.

I began my life in Florida where Mom and I were together pretty much 24/7. We went to work together, shopped together, and were at home together most of the time. We just went everywhere together, and I was sure a happy little puppy. The only real problem I had were the terrible seizures that would come on, it seemed, for no reason at all. They were awful and scared us both to death... and still do.

Something I can do, that nobody taught me, is to sit and stare for hours at a fly in the house. Eventually, it will come by me, and I can snatch it right out of the air. Like Mom says, "You gotta see it to believe it." Gramma loves that little trick of mine, and if there is a fly in the house, she makes sure I am aware of it because she can never get it with a fly swatter, so she gets it with me!

I learned early in my life that people think dogs cannot understand anything they say, but I can understand everything. I have no intention of letting anybody know that secret for fear I might have to endure learning tricks to entertain company. I don't like company and I don't like tricks, so the less Mom thinks I know, the better off I am, because I'm a mean little bastard and I like me that way.

One day Mom decided to take a trip to North Carolina to see her family, and I was treated to my first long car trip. Oh boy did we have fun.

But then we arrived, and my life was about to turn upside down. We pulled into a driveway; I got out of the car, went up on the porch and walked straight into something black, sitting there as if guarding the door. I could not bark to save my life. I had never seen anything like it, with those cold, steely eyes, and an air of complete superiority. Then, as swiftly as wind, it moved directly to me, licked my face and walked off. I peed myself. What the hell was that? And then I heard "the Gramma."

"That's Lucie's cat. The one she adopted, that I have to feed. Her name is Bowtie, and she plays with Lucie out in the yard. She sneaks up on her and attacks or she will sit on the steps, and when Lucie goes under the steps, she will reach down and pop her on the head. They just love each other to pieces."

From the voice, I just knew we were going to have some problems, so the second I entered the house I began to bark. I spotted her old calm, fat Chihuahua and immediately got right in her face and started barking and growling. Gramma told me to stop eating Lucie's face off. Mom tried her best to make me stop, but I had to let this dog know I was here now, and I am always in charge, wherever I am. Mom tossed me into my dog carrier, but Gramma said to let me loose. No caging in her house. Ah ha, I believed I was going to be in control. However, I could not have been more wrong. Gramma snatched me off the floor so fast that my toe pads were still on the rug when my butt hit the couch, rolled me upside down, put her face over mine, and said, "This is my house and I am pack leader, and if I say shut up, I mean shut the hell up. You got that?" I peed again. This was going to be a rough trip.

Gramma grabbed me up and gave me kisses all over my face just to let me know there were no hard feelings. My growl box automatically started. I don't know why, but every time anybody touches me, my growl box starts, and Gramma is always touching me just to make me crazy. She will announce my parts, one by one, and start touching me and saying, "the chin growls, the leg growls, the chest growls," and she will just go on like that for ten minutes, touching all my parts. I get meaner sounding and meaner sounding, but Gramma can sense when I've had enough and then I get grabbed up and kissed all over the face. That woman makes me insane.

Gramma had this stupid word, and still does for that matter, that means you have to go out in the yard and take care of business. She would yell, and I do mean yell, "PIPS," and every time she did, I would pee right then and there. She just scared the crap out of me. She would holler, and all my bones would just wad up and make me look like they were all broken. And then there was the eating. Just go to your bowl to get a bite to eat and you would hear, "My babies are getting some BITES. You see those good girls getting bites?" You could not even eat without the baby puppy talk going on. Bad for the digestion, I'll tell you.

By the time we left, my insides were shot; I was a total mental wreck and glad of the peace and quiet on the long ride back to Florida. I mean, she was okay, as nut cases go, but on a daily diet, Gramma could run a poor dog ragged.

All went well until the day things were being put into boxes and run out the door, and not brought back, until there was nothing left and we got into the car, with a big truck behind us and took off for parts unknown. Well, unknown until we pulled into a driveway… and guess who came out the door?

You got it: Gramma. Oh, mercy on a little dog, please. This was no visit. This was a big, new house, and we were moving in with Gramma. I would never live through this. I was a dog going downhill fast.

Here is the thing about my Mom. She can do just about anything. She can make anything, decorate anything, repair anything, and build anything. Everything hinges on desire. If she wants to do a thing, she finds out how to do it and does it. But if she has no desire to do a thing, forget it! She is not going to do it today, tomorrow, or next year. Well, with two little dogs and a big street, Mom decided we needed a fenced-in area to go PIPS. So, she just up and built a fence and boom…we had a private area. Gramma would holler PIPS, out we would go, and believe me you squatted, whether or not you had to go. If you just stood there, Gramma would leave your butt in the PIPS area till the snow fell. It was just easier to do the exercise and come back into the house without suffering any kind of humiliation. Lucie was always slow, not only because she is overweight, well, just plain fat really, but because she has to do sightseeing and visiting while she is in the yard. She talks to the neighbor dog, watches the squirrels, birds, and stray cats. I had to eat her face off every time she finally got back in because we always got a treat, and you had to wait on her balloon butt to finally get back in before treats were passed out.

I began to notice that Gramma was lying on the couch almost all the time, so to cheer her up, Lucie and I would crawl up on her and spread out on her legs. Eventually, this became a routine for us. Mom would be in her office working, and when Gramma was going on the couch, she would holler, "Going down!" and we would run hop up on her and spread out. It seemed to make her feel better, and it sure was comfortable for us. This was about the time that Gramma first saw me clean my face with my paws like a cat does. Boy did she make fun of me. She swears I have cat in my background, or I learned it from her old cat Bowtie. For some reason, I've always done this. I lick my paw and wash my face. I have a lot of facial hair, and it gets food in it and I have to clean up. What's the big deal? Don't other dogs do that?

Lucie is so fat that she cannot jump up on Gramma's bed, so she always comes to the bed and Gramma helps her up. I figured that was a little too much personal attention to suit me. So, I began to come hobbling slowly down the hall so Gramma would help me up on the bed too. "Oh, all her little bones are broken," Gramma would say, and she would reach down and pick me up and toss me on the bed. This became a routine, and to this day, if I spend the night, I still break up all my little bones to look pathetic and get helped up onto the bed.

Then one day things changed. Gramma was very sick and was taken to a hospital; she did not come back for weeks and weeks. During this time Mom met a really great man, and I liked him right away. When Gramma came home, she could no longer walk and lots of things changed. Mom fixed her house up so she could get around, then married the man, and went to live on his farm. I just adored him and was always glad to see him, but he and Mom went off a lot and I was alone. I missed my Gramma.

It was really hard to learn to tolerate the farm cows and the goats with all their weird sounds, but the real horror started when Mom began dragging stuff into the house. Outside were these things that clucked and crowed, but I could flip them off with a good vicious growl and they would run, scattering everywhere. I got a kick out of it. But it was the thing she brought into the house that just burned me up no end. She said it was a puppy, a baby dog, but the thing was larger than me. How could that be a puppy? One paw was bigger than my whole body. I barked the thing up constantly and just tore it a new face if it touched my toys. One day when I was giving it the go over, it put one of those big, gross paws on my back and flattened me right into the floor. Oh yeah, everybody laughed, funny as hell. I knew life was going to go from bad to worse as this thing grew. It took hold of one of my favorite ropes and I grabbed the other end to snatch it away, but that thing began to back up and pulled me, spread eagle, around the dining room table a dozen times. Do you think anybody rescued me and my rope? Oh no, it was every dog for himself. And that is how my life goes on the farm. Straight to hell in a dog basket.

When this monster of a dog, named Bear, was finally kicked out to protect the property, I thought that once again I would have my Mom and Dad to myself. It was so wonderful to jump up in his lap and snooze in the evening while Mom was cooking up something wonderful in the kitchen. At bedtime he would throw me up on the big bed and let me run around and growl like a rabid beast. But all good things eventually come to an end. And this end was the repeat of a horror story. Mom came home with another dog, and this time it was an Aussie that she named Sadie. This dog would learn to round up the chickens, the cows, llama, donkey, and anything else she might drag home from the auction. Once again it stayed in the house because it was a puppy, and oh how Mom adored her. Made me so mad I could not stand being in the same room with it. I got my attention from Dad. He played with me and loved on me and made me feel better. But what nobody realized was that Sadie would tear up everything. They put her in the bathroom when they went off and when they came back everything was torn down, including the curtains, toothpaste holder, shower curtains, and anything she could pry off the walls. I was so happy at the damage I knew she would be thrown out with Bear. But oh no, they had to learn the hard way, as most people do. Sadie tore up clothes, shoes, Dad's glasses, the kitchen, living room, and I just sat and watched. Nobody would ever know that I might have instigated a bit of the damage by egging her on. The day finally came when she too got tossed outside to live with Bear in the gigantic house that Mom had built especially for them. Damn thing looked like monsters lived in it, and it is on the front porch. Oh for Pete sake, it's got siding and roofing. Anybody who sees it sits in their vehicle and honks the horn. If they actually see the dogs they will decline all invites to get out.

Then the miracle happened. Somebody finally did something nice for me. I had begun to think I was lost among all the chickens and cows and dogs and everybody. I was just another one of the farm animals, not really special anymore. Believe me, I had more than a few seizures from self-pity. Then…I got my Gramma back.

Mom and Dad moved out of the little house we were in and moved into another little house of theirs, just across the street and Gramma moved into their old house. Oh, heaven above looks out for poor little doggies. Each morning when Mom and Dad go off they drop me at Gramma's house for Doggie

Day Care. Gramma is usually still in bed when we get there and I run in the door and hop up on the bed and snuggle up to her. She loves me up good and after a while we all get up, get some PIPS and treats, and Lucie and I post ourselves where we can look down the long road or just curl up in blankets and sleep. Gramma will do a few things and then pile up on the couch with us. If thunder starts, Gramma gives me a seizure pill, puts on my "thunder jacket," throws me under the covers, and snuggles up close to me so I won't be afraid. Lucie is not afraid of anything, just like Gramma, and she will sit on the back of the couch and watch the lightning and rain. She reminds me of that cat she had named Bowtie, sitting up there all calm and superior. Poor old thing got run over in the street. Mom buried it in Gramma's backyard.

Here is one really good thing about the farm: vehicles. I love to ride in Dad's big red truck, Mom's car, and best of all, the gas powered golf cart. Mom shoves me behind her back, slams her foot down and off we go with such a violent jolt that Mom's hair flies straight backward, and I cannot even wag my tail. We fly down the bumpy, rocky road, and if I knew how to laugh, this would be the time. It is really one hell of a ride and super great fun. If she comes to pick me up and she brings the golf cart, Gramma will open the porch gate and let me run out and jump on the seat to wait for Mom. I never get tired or give up. Nope, I'll sit there until the cows come home, ready and waiting, 'cause the ride is sure worth the wait.

One thing that Gramma has always respected about me was that I cannot tolerate my toe pads to get wet. And even though we always have a fenced in dog run (pips area), it is still grass, and grass gets wet. Gramma always has a special place for me to go potty where it is dry on my toe pads. She is a tough old biddy, I guess from being in the Army for so long, but she sure does love Lucie and me. She is usually pretty calm, but mess with her kids or her animals and the Sergeant comes out for the kill. And you can believe me when I say that Gramma takes no prisoners.

Gramma and I know each other very well by now. I will bark my guts out if something is wrong, and she will immediately come to see what is amiss. Lucie and I still have the job of protecting her, and when one lets out a bark, the other chimes in, even if it is Bear or Sadie, starting the ruckus in the yard. We all back each other up. But let her find that I'm barking at a chicken or a duck walking by, and its hell to pay. You gotta listen to a ten-minute lecture about the boy who cried wolf, or some such crap. I still don't like Lucie, but I can tolerate her. Actually, I don't like anybody or anything, except Mom, Dad and Gramma. But I can guarantee you that I can go out to Gramma's ramp, and if that big ass Bear and Sadie are blocking my way, I can flip them a severe growl and they will move their butts over and give me room to pass. I've made no attempt, ever, to be friends. I don't want friends; I want my people to myself. I do not share. It is not in my nature, and I do not intend to change. I was born a mean little runt and I do not intend to change my attitude for anybody. I wouldn't even if I could. I've fought hard for my nasty little reputation and I'm not giving it up to any dog, no matter how big and scary!

Well, I guess I am about finished with my sad little tale. I don't know why Gramma could not do this. She knows as much about me as I do. But, oh no, I have to tell my own story. Not that I'll ever have any descendants to read it, but the dogs that come to live here after me can get the real story. Trust nobody on a farm. At any moment they are subject to come dragging home another animal. Like the ducks. Can you believe that Gramma raised ducks and chickens, in the house, until they were big enough to go outside? And that pain-in-the-ass Lucie thought they were her babies and spent hours talking to them in some kind of baby language. It was embarrassing. Now that they are big, they are outside and she goes out on the porch and they all talk to each other. Oh, they just love her to death. It is just humiliating to have to spend every day with a dog that talks to ducks and chickens and adopts cats.

Life is just way too confusing for a "precious" little dog like me. Oh well, I'll muddle through it all somehow.

THE DISAPPEARANCE

Some people move to small towns because they want to have a comfortable life where neighbors know one another, get together, have town celebrations, and work together for the betterment of the town. These kinds of towns are not for the city slickers who want meaningless excitement, never know their neighbors, and only attend celebrations sponsored and worked by someone else. People like Joan and Jim Angel and their 5-year-old son Marcus moved to Creek City because it drew them with the gorgeous farms, quaint little town with novelty shops, and homes that were spread out right from the town area. The parks all had little creeks where the children could remove their shoes and wade in the water and pick up little stones of all colors. There were only 3 schools, one for each level: grammar, middle and high school. The kids grew up together, had activities together, and chose their little groups when becoming teens. It was the easy way to grow up, without terrorism in the schools, ridiculous rules about cough drops, or bullies who beat kids to death while being egged on by other students. The Angels could not picture their son having to grow up being scared out of his wits every school day of the year. Marcus was a genius and would surely be singled out each and every day by jealous dimwits. It was unthinkable to put a talented child through hell for twelve years... or however few it took him to graduate. Marcus needed private tutoring, but he also needed some social interaction in his life, so the schools agreed to start him out in the first grade and, as he conquered everything the teacher could teach him, move him on to second grade and continue until he graduated at whatever age he was when he had learned all they could possibly teach him and he had achieved all his necessary credits.

A wonderful life faced the Angels, and they began to join in the community activities little by little. Marcus was a wonderful child to know. He liked to look at all sides of a problem, discuss each, and come to the decision that seemed most logical. He had long talks with grownups, getting their ideas and opinions about politics, wars, the law, and every important subject he could think would interest him. He had conversations with the pastors, farmers, lawyers, and one day with the town sheriff. He had discovered that the sheriff had been a policeman in New York at one time and wanted him to share some of the worst crimes he had worked. They sat down in the soda shop and over milkshakes the sheriff told him all the things that he felt were fitting for a little boy's ears, but Marcus realized he was leaving out the good parts.

"Marcus, what is it you value most in your life?"

"The love of my mother and father I value above all else in life!"

"Good boy," he said. And with that they parted ways.

Joan had nearly died giving birth to Marcus, and the doctor told her she would never be able to have another child. Jim and Marcus both knew she could not have a child and never anticipated the miracle that occurred when the little genius turned thirteen. It was a difficult pregnancy and a worse delivery, but Joan lived through both and became the proud mother of a baby girl. There were showers and gifts of all kinds for two very proud parents. The home was rearranged to accommodate the little girl and their brains were worn out trying to think of an appropriate name for their new Angel. They finally decided upon Precious Angel and both agreed that it was perfect. Marcus did not vote. He resented having another child in the family, and did not care what they called her as the baby was *theirs* and they could pick any name they wanted. He wanted nothing to do with any of it at all.

The evening all the rearrangements had been finished on the house and they were ready to announce the little girl's name, they had a backyard barbecue. It was a wonderful yard for a party because it backed up to woods about a quarter of a mile thick, behind their house, and extended from their backyard down to the highway about two miles away, and up the side of their house, being the last house on that road. It was an open invitation to everybody on the street to bring a dish or hotdogs and buns, whatever they had handy, and come on over for a hoedown. They had some fiddles going, dozens of lawn chairs sitting everywhere, people showing up with boxes and boxes of meats and drinks, and there was so much happiness that nobody even noticed when the baby disappeared from the house. About 7:30 Jim announced that he was going to get the child and they would like all their friends to join in the naming of the little girl. He walked into the house, but was running back out screaming like a lunatic saying that the baby was not in her crib. It was yelled that maybe one of the old ladies had picked her up and was walking her or rocking her and everybody rushed around trying to find the baby. Joan was hysterical and could not be comforted by anybody. Marcus came over and hugged his mother and said, "You will always have me to look out for you." She hugged him back even though his words could not ease her agony; she felt he was trying to take some of her grief away and that meant a great deal to her.

The sheriff was at the barbecue, and he immediately took charge. He wanted to know if anybody had seen a person that he did not know or had not seen before. After that was settled he asked everybody to spread out and go a few yards into the woods just to see if there were any footprints or anything suspicious. Neighbors ran home for flashlights before anybody started out, but after a thorough search, nobody found anything suspicious.

The doctor was called and gave Joan a shot to help her sleep for a few hours, but he assured Jim that he was about to face a tough time with Joan. If the baby was kidnapped and still alive, there was a chance to get her back, but the sheriff also had said that if it was a pedophile crime then the baby was most likely not going to be found alive. He and Joan were facing a nightmare.

Nobody called the house asking for a ransom and after six months, they knew they would never see their little girl again. They were each other's strength during the next few years and focused all their attention on their wonderful son. There had been no parties in a long time, and they decided it was time to give Marcus a party for his graduation. He was in charge of the guest list and sent out formal invitations to about a hundred students. There was to be a game in the backyard that would be talked about for many years and probably generations. The game was to be cute, simple, and fun. Nobody ever dreamed that midway through the game, another nightmare would attack the Angel family.

After everybody ate and danced for a few songs, Marcus announced that now that it was dusk, they were all to go into the woods and search for the golden egg. Colored eggs were everywhere, hundreds of them, but there was only one golden egg, and the prize in the egg was worth every bit of trouble they would have finding it in its little hiding place. He had a box of Halloween lights that when popped, lit up, so everybody grabbed a few and began to hunt. There were yellow ribbons tying off the area where they could hunt so that nobody would get lost or hurt. Some of the guys picked up big sticks and began to prod the trees and move dead leaves around on the ground, but none of them picked up the colored eggs; that was just too girly for them. They were after the golden egg. There was a little group of kids together, three girls and two guys, giggling and teasing each other by poking with sticks and just having a good time. One of the girls said that she saw something yellow in a tree and the boys began prodding like crazy with their sticks. The piercing scream came first from the mouth of the girl upon whom the skeleton fell: then all three girls were hysterical and the yells were like those of injured animals. The horror of what was at their feet was so overwhelming that the boys could not control them or get them to move.

Jim came crashing through the trees and when he saw the bones of his child, still in her baby clothes, wrapped tightly in her yellow blanket, but a skeleton, he fell to his knees and scooped her up into his arms. He told the boys to get the sheriff and to make everybody go home and for somebody to get a neighbor to stay with Joan, but not to let her come into the woods.

In about ten minutes the sheriff found Jim sitting against a tree rocking his baby and softly telling her that they had done everything they could to find her and had loved her every single day since she had disappeared. Joan was right behind him. A team of wild horses could not have kept her from her baby. She took the child in her arms and swore that she would find the culprit and rip out his throat herself. The sheriff noticed that the tree could actually be climbed and he got up into the branches to see if he could tell where the child had been laid to rest. She had been tied to the branch so as not to fall on the ground and be found. Carefully, he examined the rope holding the baby in place, and horror took hold of him as he realized who had killed the little girl. He remembered the search and people looking on the ground for evidence, but who would have looked up? It would take a very clever killer to plan this crime. And then he remembered something from many years ago. He remembered a conversation with a little boy whom he had asked a question… and he remembered the answer. At the time he thought it an incredible comment from a child. Now he realized that it had a double-edged meaning. *The love of my mother and father I value above all else.* He never intended to let another child share in that love that belonged to him and him alone.

Every murderer who thinks he has committed the perfect crime finds a need to brag about his cleverness, and Marcus was no different. He just had to prove that nobody would discover the skeletonized remains that he had tied so securely to the tree branch high enough in the tree that it could not be seen from the ground. He never dreamed that a six foot boy with a long stick would be prodding the tree and loosen the rope enough for the baby to fall. Naturally, the rope was originally tied around muscle and when there was no longer any flesh, the rope could no longer hold the baby if it was jostled.

The sheriff took the child and told Jim and Joan that she would be seen by the doctor, and then sent to the funeral home, and at last they could have their child's service. He told them he would take Marcus with him so he could ask him some questions about the other kids at the party. As he went through the yard, with the baby in his arms, he took Marcus by the arm and told him to come with him. He would need somebody to hold the baby while he drove. It was the worst thing he could legally do to Marcus aside from shooting him in the face, which is exactly what he wanted to do the second he realized who had killed the baby. Anybody who killed a defenseless baby was not a human being, but a monster without a conscience.

After leaving the remains with the doctor, they went to the jailhouse. Marcus asked him why he was not taking him back home and with great pleasure, the sheriff slapped the cuffs on him and told him he was under arrest for murder. Being alone in the police station he was not taking any chances on a fight with Marcus and he knew that if the boy ran, he would just shoot him in the back. Naturally, Marcus professed his innocence and demanded he be released. Marcus cursed the sheriff for the idiot he was and told him there was absolutely no evidence as to his guilt and his parents would sue him and the city if he did not release him immediately. The sheriff let him know that Joan intended to rip out the throat of the person who murdered her baby and the sheriff thought it might be a good idea to keep him away from his mother. Marcus laughed and said his mother would never hurt him for any reason; he was her pride and joy. Her *only* pride and joy.

Secretly the sheriff praised jailhouse conversations being taped. He was the proud owner of the whole setup-visual and audio, and he intended to have Marcus hang himself. As the sheriff prodded Marcus, he responded just like any other killer. He was so careful and so perfect and nobody would ever be able to prove a thing against him. He told the sheriff that DNA was everything today and circumstantial evidence would never convict him of anything. Just as the sheriff had told him years ago, if a body remains in the open for years, chances of any DNA being available was practically nil. And if a member of a family was guilty, there was no way to prove that his DNA had gotten there by any means other than everyday handling of everything in the house. It was a nightmare case to prove.

"Marcus, I found the rope. Remember the rope that you should have gone back and removed after all the searches were over? It was the same rope I had given to you when I showed you how to tie some different kinds of knots. It was the rope you carried around for weeks trying out different new knots you thought up, and those knots are still in the rope." Marcus screamed at the top of his lungs, not at the sheriff, but at his own negligence and oversight. He never made mistakes, not ever, not for any reason whatsoever. As he was screaming, the sheriff shoved him into the jail cell and locked the door.

"Damn her for getting pregnant, damn him for getting her pregnant, damn the baby for being born. This was supposed to be *my* life and *my life alone.* They ruined everything!" He was screaming these obscenities at the top of his lungs.

Marcus heard a sound and turned around to see his parents standing in the doorway of his jail cell. They both looked as though they had just stumbled across a horrible scene that their brains could not process, and both faces were totally blank. Marcus reached through the bars towards them, but Jim just took Joan's arm, turned her around and walked her out the door. He reached behind himself and pulled the door closed.

"Do you stay here all night, Sheriff Johnson?"

"Normally, with a prisoner, one of us would stay, either me or the deputy. But he is out of town and I'm too tired, so I guess I will be going home. He is not going to say anything else, so I'm just going to take the tape with me, and I'll come back in the morning to bring him some breakfast."

"Thank you for all your help, your intelligence, and your compassionate heart." And with that, Jim took Joan home.

After getting Joan to sleep with the help of sleeping pills, Jim loaded his truck with a couple of cans of gasoline, matches and his hunting knife. When he arrived at the jailhouse, the door was unlocked, as expected, and Jim entered with his heavy heart and a prayer to please forgive him. Nothing so evil could live, and Joan was not going to witness the trial of her beloved son who had killed her precious little baby. He took the keys to the cell door, quietly unlocked it, and stood over his son... watching him sleep. The boy opened his eyes and smiled up at his Dad as though he had come there to take him home. Jim cut his throat from ear to ear as he said, "I brought you something from your Mother."

Leaving him there to die, Jim closed the cell door, replaced the key and began to slosh gasoline throughout the little jailhouse. He tossed the match, cried, and went home.

Jim fixed the coffee and made sure that Joan came down for breakfast. He wanted her there in time to see the Morning News. It was the first story, and the Sheriff was being interviewed. He was saying that he was blessed that he had the foresight to take the tapes home with him or they would be lost as well. He could only figure that somebody had hated the Angel boy so much that he used this crime as an excuse to kill him. Nothing this awful had ever happened in this town, and it was likely that anybody could have burned down the jail with him inside. There was no evidence pointing at anybody, so he was not going to waste taxpayers' money searching through a tunnel of confusion with no light at the end of the tunnel. What he needed to concentrate on now was building a new jailhouse with a few up-to-date features to preclude any such thing ever happening again. The matter was closed.

Joan was crying her heart out that her son had burned to death. "No matter what he did, he was obviously mentally ill and did not deserve to burn to death." Jim turned to her and said that she was the one who said that she would tear out the throat of the man who killed her baby. Then he added, "He was dead when I burned down the jail."

Joan moved to his lap so they could hug and cry together, and they sat there for half an hour. Jim told her that he could not bear to stay in this house or in this town after losing his children in such horrible ways, and they needed to go somewhere else and try to find some solace.

They both got meaningless jobs, went to celebrations set up by some fund or the city, lived in an apartment where they did not know their neighbors, and did not even care. They ate in a different restaurant every Saturday night and pretended it was date night. They never went to church again as they both felt so guilty, of so much, and their lives got more and more hollow every day.

One Sunday morning a little stranger called at their door, and when Joan opened it she passed out cold. The girl began to scream and Jim came running. He saw Joan on the floor and paid no attention to the girl. He fell to his knees and pulled Joan into his arms. As she slowly opened her eyes, she pointed up to the girl, and Jim's eyes rested on his wife at a young age of about 10. The girl had a letter in her hand, which she gave to Jim without a word. He read it out loud.

My baby girl died just about the time your little girl was born. Marcus hated your baby, so it was easy to convince him to put my little girl in your baby's clothes and give your baby to me. I have been very good to her and have loved her to pieces, but I'm about to die and have to make my peace with God and her parents. I give this wonderful child back to you and even though I'm sorry for what I've done, there is no way I can make up for the years you lost with this precious child. Tears were running down the child's face as she stood there listening to her mother's admission of guilt and wondering if these people would want her back after all these years.

"Mama told me all about what she did. She was wonderful to me. I really want to go home."

Joan jumped up and grabbed the child into her arms and Jim joined in with arms spread around both his girls. Choking on her sobs, she said, "Your name is Precious Angel."

"That's what my Mom always called me, and I thought it was so beautiful. I'm sorry she is going to die, because I love her very much."

"We will do the best we can for you Precious, and hope that in time you will come to love us just as much as you loved her."

"Do you live here, in this awful city?"

"Oh no dear, we were just here for a short time. We are going to find a nice, quiet, safe little town where the children are safe and the living is easy, where you know your neighbors and have a great many friends."

The story of their lives began again, in another town, with a beautiful daughter who was just as normal as a girl could be, with only one outstanding gift to her credit: she sang like an angel.

Sheriff Johnson got his new jail with some very nice features, such as a small fireplace. Sitting directly in the middle of the mantel is a golden egg, without its contents of course. In climbing the tree, he had spotted the egg on a branch of the next tree, went back later to retrieve it, and was amazed to find that it held $1,000. He gave it to the mortician to finish the cremation of Marcus, put him in a vase with babies on it, and buried it in the woods next to the tree where the baby was found. Every time he looked at the treasure it reminded him that people are always searching for their own personal golden egg, never realizing that they have already found it in family.

FLOWER

Allison was huffing and puffing just as hard as she could, and Mark was saying all the encouraging things he was supposed to say while trying not to faint. The doctor told her to give a couple of good pushes and they would have themselves a baby. All of a sudden, she heard, "Put her to sleep." Out she went and did not wake up until evening.

After she blinked a couple of times to focus her eyes, she turned and saw Mark with his head between his hands. She called his name, and when he looked up she could see the pain and agony in his face. Her heart gave a lunge. She did not want to ask the one question. Once you ask and get an answer, there is no turning back…you cannot change a thing. She could not face him, so she looked away, as though that would make all the grief she felt completely vanish.

"Allison, the baby is not dead. She is just, well, different." He pressed the call button to let the doctor know that she was awake. He did not have the ability to tell his wife what was wrong with their baby girl, and really, he did not know any more than the doctor, which was basically nothing. All they knew was what they saw.

Dr. Reynolds came in with the baby wrapped up in a beautiful pink blanket. He did not hand the baby to Allison, but held her in his arms.

"This is cruel, I know, but first we talk, and then, if you want to see your baby, you can. I have never seen anything like this, nor have I even heard of such a thing occurring. I've called every specialist in the world that might have encountered such a birth, but they were just as shocked as I. You have to make a decision now, and very quickly, because I've made a terrible mistake in asking for help. If you want to keep your child, then you must take her and go right now, and if you do not wish to keep her, you must go anyway. When the media gets ahold of this case, and you can be sure that they will, doctors will do everything in their power to take the child. She will become an experiment, and you will never see her again. If they gain all the information they need and the child is of no further use to them, she will go straight to an institution and there she will die. She will never be released. I do not believe she will live very long, so if you have any place that is relatively quiet and safe, I suggest you take your child and go there."

"Tell me what is wrong with her before I look. I do not want her to hear rejection in my voice or see it in my eyes when I take her in my arms."

"She is old. Perhaps 100 years old or more. She has arthritis and hardening of the arteries. She is nearly blind, and I think she is deaf. It appears that she lived an entire lifetime in your womb. You will not be able to nurse her as she has a full set of teeth. Do you want to see her?"

"Of course, she is my baby and my responsibility. I would never turn my back on a child I created. Whatever is wrong with her is our fault, and we will love her until she dies."

Mark, to whom nobody had spoken, jumped up and grabbed Allison's robe and the wheelchair he had already gotten ready, just in case. His demeanor changed from that of a despondent father into a man with a mission. He was taking charge, and he would protect his two girls. When he first saw the baby at birth, he nearly fainted. After Allison was asleep he was able to scream out his questions to the doctor, but quickly discovered that nobody in the delivery room had ever seen such a baby. He had become a father in charge of a dying child, and with deep remorse and grief he knew he would have to hold this child until she died. She could not die alone and unloved. If Allison did not want the baby, then he would have to go somewhere to hold the child himself, alone. He could only think of one place where he and the child could go to be safe from prying eyes.

Allison reached for her child, hugged her close to her chest, pulled the blanket back, and kept the shudders from herself and her child by telling her that she understood how much was lost to her, but in the time they had together she would show her all about love. "You are like a beautiful flower that has closed up at night. In the evening it is all shriveled up, protecting the glorious radiance of what's inside, and come the morning, the flower will burst open and just take your breath away. Your name is Flower. You represent all the lovely flowers in the world, just waiting to display all their beauty along with all your inner beauty. Let's go Daddy. Little Flower needs a new home."

For the first time in his practice, Dr. Reynolds sat down and cried the very moment they left the room. He had just been through the worst experience of his life, and he did not wish to ever see another child born in this condition. He would love to know what caused this creation, just as much as the other doctors who would be calling and coming, demanding to know all that he knew. He had gleaned all the information from the records that would be pertinent to diagnosis, but he then had destroyed every record, every computer entry that mentioned the family name. As far as an investigator could go was that a child was born to an unknown woman, was examined, and then disappeared from the hospital. How all the entries and paperwork managed to disappear he would say baffled him as well, and he could only imagine that the father wanted privacy--to which he was certainly entitled--and saw that he got it by getting rid of the records. The doctor would do absolutely nothing to help anybody find the family.

Mark's brother had already arranged for a moving van and it was in the driveway when they arrived. Paying them extra and instructing them to pack everything and store it until it was called for, he and Allison took only clothes and the baby things with them when they left. He stopped at his brother's home, traded cars with him, and headed for West Virginia. His Uncle Tobie had left him a cabin in the mountains, which he had never visited and never seen. He had owned it for several years, but had never bothered to go there as he imagined it was some old beat-up shack that was probably ready to fall down, but he told Allison that they were going there to see if they could sell the property and get enough money to go away somewhere until Flower passed on and they could return.

Funny how the best laid plans just never go the way one expects them to… mainly because we are never in control of our fate, but we always live as though we are.

They spent one night in a motel, and Allison was pleased to have the rest. They rocked Flower and told her about all the beautiful things she would see in the woods. She never cried, drank very little formula, and seemed quite content to just sleep. Riding seemed to soothe her because she looked as though she were smiling all the time. It was a most pleasant trip, but when they arrived at the *cabin*, they were shocked! They had to be at the wrong address because before them stood a log cabin two floors high with a screened-in porch that went all the way around the house. Mark just laughed and said he would go ask the people who lived there where his property might be and how to get there. He left Allison in the car chuckling and delighted to feel so light hearted.

The old man that answered the door had a grin spread wide across his face when he saw Mark. "Well, well, it's about time son. I'm your uncle's nephew, Tommy, and he left me in charge of this here mansion until you showed up. He is getting a good laugh about now because he said you would take years to come and look because he knew that you would just think it was an old shack. Oh, is he getting a good laugh now."

"This beautiful home is mine? You have to be kidding!"

"Get your family on in here and I'll show you around. He left you some other stuff too, but said I could never tell you anything until you showed up."

Mark went out to the car and told Allison that they had arrived. She just stared at him as though her husband had lost his mind, but she did as he asked and got Flower and they went into their home. Tommy hugged Allison but did not comment on the baby at all. He just asked them to sit down for a quick chat and then he would go and leave them to get settled. He brought iced tea and little cookies, and began to speak without any further niceties.

"Child was born old, right?" They were both shocked at the question and neither answered, but Allison hugged Flower even closer. "No matter, it's happened up here before. It's in the family and we got a picture album here that you can look at later and that will give you some hope for the baby's future. She isn't going to die, if that is what they told you. Nope, she was just born on the wrong end of life. What will be the hardest for you to cope with is the fact that she will get younger and eventually become a baby, and *that* is when she will die. You can never leave these mountains with her as folks up here know what to do with her if something happens to you two. See, you will get older, and she will get younger, and if you die, she has to be taken care of by those who know what is happening. You are here to stay!" Tommy then told them that every dollar Mark's uncle had saved was not in a bank but right here in this house. There was an old trunk in the attic that had the family albums and the money and some rare items found on the property that would be worth a great deal. "Something is wrong in our family, Mark. This happens from time to time, but for the children who go off to find a better life, out of the mountains, we never tell them for fear it will frighten them out of ever having kids. It does not happen often, and there is no set pattern to allow us to know who is next. When it happens, we deal with it and help each other. Your uncle was afraid for *you*, for some reason, so he saved and built so that one day you would have a place to run if you needed to hide. And here you are! He trusted me to take care of everything because he knew I would live a long time. I too was born old. I look about 70, but I'm really only 30 years old." Neither Mark nor Allison could speak. And with that, Tommy turned and walked out of the door.

Mark and Allison were on an emotional rollercoaster, not knowing what to do first, so they decided to do everything one step at a time. First they needed to tour the house and see what they had to live with…what room would be the baby's…whether or not there were any supplies. They began with the kitchen and found no food in either the huge refrigerator or the cabinets. Next, they looked in the dining room and the little room that was obviously an office space with a small bathroom. Then, they went upstairs to find two huge bedrooms, side by side, each with a walk-in closet and a bathroom. One was outfitted for a woman and the other for a man. Allison was delighted as she joked how she could throw him out when he snored or just got on her nerves. After a quick hug and kiss, they looked in the small room across the hall and found the most precious nursery imaginable, and next to this, obviously a child's playroom, but outfitted with a rocking chair, a wheelchair, crutches, and various other pieces of equipment for an elderly person. In the walk-in closet were dozens of toys wrapped in cellophane to preserve them until needed. Then they understood. We have grownup rooms for a man and a woman, depending on which our child might be and a nursery for when it's needed and everything Flower needs while she descends the aging ladder.

There was a knock on the door, which then opened by itself and several men came in, calling out to Mark that they brought the groceries, already paid for by Tommy. Allison laid the baby in the crib, and they went downstairs to find boxes and boxes of food and baby needs piled on the dining room table. They all waved and said they would hope to see them soon in the store, and off they went. Allison gasped at the volume of food, and Mark suggested they hire that team back to put it all away. They both got such a good laugh that all their built-up tension just evaporated as tears rolled down their cheeks. When they got hold of themselves, they went into the kitchen to begin putting things away and found a roasted chicken and several casseroles on the kitchen counter. They could not believe the kindnesses that had come their way and knew that they would have to find a way to pay everyone back one way or another.

They packed the refrigerator and cabinets and then sat down at their new dining room table to enjoy their first decent meal in a very long time. They were happy, settled, already had friends, and knew that none of these people would give them away and would probably go a very long way to protect them from the outside should they come looking for them... which, of course, they did.

The intake clerk at the hospital remembered their names, and she had one piece of evidence that had been overlooked: the hospital bracelet. She had errors on the first one she made, had crammed it into her pocket--so as not to be caught, and had remade the bracelet correctly. She was new and on probation for 90 days, and feared this mistake would count heavily against her when she was evaluated.

Everybody got briefed about talking to anybody about patients, and she began to wonder what was so secretive. When she got home that night she discovered the forgotten bracelet in the pocket of her sweater and she wondered if this was by any chance a "gold mine" mistake, so she kept it and placed it in a drawer. Sure enough, in a couple of months people were snooping around trying to get information. One guy came up to her desk and asked her what she knew about a strange birth in the hospital; jokingly she asked him what it was worth to him. When he said that this was the story of a lifetime and it was worth one million dollars, she nearly had a heart attack on the spot. The arrangement was made. She cashed the check, turned over the bracelet, quit her job, and disappeared.

Now all the foxes had a trail to follow, and they were relentless. They found Mark and Allison's old home, which was up for sale, not by the owners, but by Dean, the brother with a Power of Attorney. When they descended on Dean, they found an irate man who cursed them all for the idiots that they were.

"Are you people insane? My brother and his wife gave birth to a precious little girl who only lived for two days. They privately had her cremated and have gone away to try to recover from their loss. And you animals want to make their loss of a child even more unbearable because you sense there may be a story in it somehow? You make me sick. Don't you ever come on my property again, or I swear I will start shooting as soon as I open the door!"

"I guess I'll have to go out and buy you a gun today if you are going to start shooting people," said his wife and they both laughed and headed for the kitchen and a cup of tea.

Nobody could have found Mark and Allison by searching titles because the house and property were all in Tommy's name for just this very reason: people hunting for them. Tommy also had a will leaving everything to Mark, just in case. He came over one evening and explained everything to them so they would not worry. He told them he would be around to help Flower come down from old to new until he was too little to understand anymore what was going on, but by then she would know how to deal with everything going on in her life. She really should never marry as she would continue to get young and her husband would get older and certainly there was too great a chance she would give birth to children like herself. Tommy thought he was the last and vowed never to reproduce in order to protect a future problem, but Uncle Tobie was very suspicious about Mark and concerned about his lineage, therefore protecting him just in case he fathered an oldster.

As the years went by, life became so pleasant that it felt as if they had been overly blessed. There were dozens and dozens of families from one extreme to the other, hidden throughout the mountains, just as in any normal American town. There were old guys running stills and running from the law. There were lumberjacks who doubled as firefighters, prosperous families and poor families, but the one thing that made them different was that they closed ranks against outsiders and would truly kill to protect one of their own. Townspeople told a story about a news media truck that came rolling into town around thirty years ago, and when the driver parked in front of the only café, forty men with rifles blocked their way. They got in their van to leave, and a caravan followed them all the way to the county line. Nobody ever came back. They had heard a rumor about Tommy, and there was no doubt that the newsmen and their van would disappear and anybody revealing the secret right along with them. It's just an old mountain code: He who tells, dies!

At one point in their lives, Flower was nearly the age of her parents, and this caused a great deal of happiness and laughter all around. But everybody was well aware that as they passed one another, they were going to reverse in roles. Flower was just like any other child growing up, except for the fact that she looked different. At some point she would have to begin making adult decisions, even though she looked as though she had been doing so for a very long time. Mark, Allison and Tommy knew her very well and knew at what stage of her life she needed to be given less advice as a child, and more consideration as an adult.

One day, Flower would be taking care of her parents and wanted to take care of Tommy, as well, but as yet she had no idea who would take care of her. This was a puzzle for them all that stayed in the back of their heads.

One evening Tommy came over to have a serious talk; nobody liked the sound of it and feared what might be coming. He explained that even though oldsters look about a hundred when they are born, some are much younger, just as some people who look young at 65 and others look 85. Nobody knew at what age oldsters started out, so there was never any idea how old they were at any given time. He knew how long he had been living, but he did not know how old he was in "regular" people years. He had begun to change a great deal in a short time: he found himself flirting with girls, beer tasted good, and such things were coming on all the time. It had been so many years that he knew nobody was looking for them now, so he went ahead and put the home and property in their names, all three of them. He felt that he had been a lot younger than Flower when he was born and now was probably approaching teenage years because he was acting just like all the teens around town. Mark and Allison were devastated, even though they had always known this day would come. Flower just sat there and cried at the thought of losing her lifetime friend.

We all know the stages of life, but we are never prepared when they arrive.

"Don't you ask anybody to take care of you Tommy. I owe you my life, and you are my very best friend, after Mama and Daddy, so you just have to depend on us, please."

"I'll be just fine until about twelve or so, and then I'll get scared because I won't know how to do anything. Unfortunately, we don't bring our knowledge with us as you do when you go the other way. We keep forgetting things, just as though we have Alzheimer's. You will have to keep an eye out for me and when I'm lost, you come and find me, and I will live with you as your adopted child. Are you sure that will be all right?"

"Oh please," said Mark. "You have been our trusted friend all these many years. We have to take care of each other, because if we don't, then who will look out for us?"

"And who will look out for Flower? She will be last, and there is no other family or friend to take care of her. What will she do then?"

Flower spoke up and answered Tommy, as though she had been giving it a great deal of consideration for a long time. She explained that she was going to turn the house into a home for the elderly, with the specific exception that if an oldster were to be born, he/she would be welcome here in the old age, down through the youth and into death. If they were here during the years when they were old, then this would be the only place to come back to in their youth when they needed help once again. Tommy grabbed her and hugged her so hard she thought her ribs would crack.

"Flower, I'm going to sell everything I have and put the money in the trunk for your future home. Then I am going off to have a bit of adventure before I forget how. I'll be back when I realize I can no longer drive that old heap of mine."

Everybody hugged all around and wished Tommy a happy time and a safe return. Nobody was really elated by these events because it signaled changes were coming that could not be faced without a lot of heartache and agony, but Flower's idea for the home was the most sensible that could ever have been devised. She would never be alone, and the home would protect others in the future, and very probably, there would be others. Not everybody in the mountains wanted to or could afford to take proper care of oldsters. None were ever passed off or neglected, but their care sometimes left a lot to be desired. Now they all had a future, and the problem remained in the mountains where it belonged. People in the mountains were all related in one way or another, so nobody ever knew who might be next to give birth to an oldster. It did not happen often, but when it did, the generation that received the oldster had to have been prepared through family knowledge being passed down, and they needed options. Flower was giving the future oldsters at least one good option when there were no others.

One morning, a few years later, Flower took her coffee out on the porch to sit and enjoy the early morning. There in a corner of the porch, she found a boy of about 12 curled up in a ball crying his eyes out. She bent down and picked him up, wiped his face with her handkerchief, and asked him if he knew his name.

"Course I know my name, do I look like an idiot? I was just cold and wanted to stay here until it warmed up outside. Now let me go."

"And what if I had pancakes with maple syrup and milk in the kitchen. Do you think you would have enough time to eat before you go?" He shrugged and guessed he could, and from then on Tommy lived in the home with lots of love and lots of toys. Flower saw herself and prayed that the ones who took care of her would be as kind to her.

As the years passed, Tommy became a little boy, then a baby and one afternoon, snuggled against Flower he slipped away. She buried him in the rose garden.

Mark died of a heart attack, leaving his women to make everything work without his wonderful guidance and patience. Doing him proud, Flower turned the home into a place for the aged and created stipulations about the oldsters. Nobody could ever work in the home unless they were raised in these mountains and held the same honors about closing ranks. The old folks coming here had to have been raised in the mountains so they could continue to take care of their own.

Allison got to meet the people who would be in charge of the home, and she was quite satisfied. They cared for her until her death, and she got an opportunity to braid the hair of her little girl. Soon after Allison passed away, Flower caught the flu and died. They were both buried in the family plot in the rose garden, along with Mark and Tommy.

The woman in charge of the three old ladies, mountain women who had come to live there, was Marian Moore and she was devoted completely to their care and their happiness. There was a young girl who did the cleaning, a middle aged woman who cooked, and her husband was the gardener. They were all from the mountains.

Marian made special evenings when she would teach the old ladies to play a game or play one they knew. During one of these evenings there was a knock on the door and when she answered, a young man and his wife stepped inside with a baby in their arms.

"Before you send us away, please hear me out. Mark had a brother, and his brother had a son, and I am *his* son. We have always known about the oldsters in the family, but nobody ever really believed it or gave birth to one. Not until now. This place, this address was always attached to our birth certificates, or in our favorite books, anywhere that our fathers thought we might find it, and all it said was that an oldster is to be taken to Flower's home. Nobody ever met Flower, and really we all thought it was just a story, but when John was born, suddenly, at home, I knew we had to run. All the stories came back to me, and I knew he would be an experiment. Nobody can know about him. Please believe me. We have two other children who are in high school and we are both teachers. We can't keep him. There is just no way to keep him safe.

"We've been waiting for you, boy. Come and see him any time you want to, but live your life well and never worry about the child. Flower made sure that he would be taken care of properly, and look at the lovely ladies who will enjoy his company."

They all talked for a while and took turns holding the infant while his room was prepared. And so, the cycle began again… as it probably would many times in the future.

THE LIFE I HAVE CHOSEN
By
Mary Suzanne Pebworth McKinney
Written many, many years ago

Here I am,
in the life I have chosen.
Day in, day out – clichés at every turn,
in more stress than is comfortable for me.
I lash out and hate myself for it.
Forgiveness comes slowly.
Why have I come to this?
It was supposed to be different;
_I_ was supposed to be different.
Again I find myself in a warm tub,
gently soaking away the discomfort in my soul.
Quietly, the little voice filters through the door,
"Mommy, will you rock me?"
A warmth penetrates my mind;
the mood has passed.
I am a mother. I am a wife.
Cradling the child, I rock and hum
a slow steady rhythm.
Here I am,
in the life I have chosen.

ALTERNATE LIFE

When Dr. Overman walked into the hospital room of Doris Kline, age 73, a young woman was sitting by the bed, talking and crying. She was holding Mrs. Kline's hand, pleading for her grandmother to wake up and return to her.

"Are you Mary Scott, her granddaughter?"

"Yes," she replied, without looking up at the doctor. She knew her eyes were red and swollen and her mind was so perplexed about her grandmother's condition that she could not endure any conversation with anyone.

"According to her file, you are her only living relative. Is that correct?"

"Yes."

"I am Dr. Overman, a specialist in coma conditions, and I've been evaluating your grandmother. We need to have a very serious talk."

Mary stood up and faced the doctor. "Are you going to tell me the same thing I've heard over and over again, that you have no idea what is wrong with her?" Her face was red and hot and she was ready to do battle with the next doctor who told her that he knew absolutely nothing.

"This is the fourth time she has gone into a coma. She is causing this herself."

Her temper flared, and she yelled, "Are you crazy?" There was something physically or mentally wrong with her grandmother, but she was certainly not deliberately causing herself to go into a coma, knowing full well that her granddaughter would be scared to death, just as she was the last three times.

"Look very carefully at your grandmother's face. Do you see her eyelids moving as though she is dreaming?"

"So...?"

"Her eyelids move constantly, something nobody does when asleep. Nobody dreams like that in a coma. You need to come with me."

Dr. Overman led Mary on a long walk through winding hallways until they approached a guarded door. When it was unlocked, they proceeded through two more sets of locked doors opened first by voice control and second by handprint. Mary was becoming more and more afraid. In fact, she was rapidly approaching *terrified*. They entered a covered walkway about a full block long that led to a free-standing building she had never noticed from the street.

"What is this place?" she said with a very shaky voice.

"This is the Dream Coma Center, and what I am about to show you is not to be discussed with anyone, for any reason, outside this building. Do you understand me?"

"Yes."

"We will be going into a room now where all the patients are in a dream coma. I want you to look at their faces very carefully, and tell me the difference between them and your grandmother."

They walked into a room such as Mary had never seen before in her young life, nor would have ever been able to imagine. There were no fewer than 100 hammocks in the room, each suspended by two posts, and each holding a human being.

"What is this place, and what is wrong with all these people?"

"Do as I asked you, and look directly and carefully at their faces."

Mary reluctantly did as she was instructed and walked slowly forward to look at the first person. The eyelids were moving as though they were dreaming, and the lips were sucked inward as though clenched down by the teeth and held in place. Mary reached a hand forward and touched the bare arm; it was ice cold. She could not help but move to the next body and then the next, until she was satisfied that all of them were in the same condition. She felt the tears sliding down her face. She just knew that the doctor was going to place her grandmother in one of these hammocks very soon and that was why he had brought her here.

"What's wrong with them?"

"Come with me and we will talk."

Dr. Overman took her by the arm and led her down the hallway to a pleasant little room with couches and cold bottled water, for which she was very grateful. A little went down her throat and a little went on a handkerchief which she then wiped over her face. Whatever they were about to discuss was going to be just horrible, and she felt that every second she delayed might somehow change the outcome of the conversation.

"Please sit down, Mary, because what I am about to explain to you is going to be very difficult for you to understand. Are you a Christian, Mary? By that, I mean do you believe in God?"

"My grandmother raised me in the church, and I can't imagine a life without her or God."

"I'm glad to hear that because what I think is happening is better understood if you are a Christian. We are always worried about doing evil and losing our souls to the devil, but many Christians believe that God or Jesus can be called upon even at the time of death. We can be saved by confessing our sins and asking him for forgiveness. Christians make it very difficult for the devil to gain souls…souls of good people. I am very afraid that the devil has found a new way to steal good souls from God."

"What on earth are you talking about? Are all those people in the hammocks dead, or at least brain dead? Is that why their skin is so cold?

"Let me begin at the beginning. About 2 years ago I was called upon to examine a young man who was in a coma. There was no accident of any kind to cause his condition and tests showed nothing wrong with his brain. However, now that it can be determined when somebody is dreaming, we realized that he was dreaming around the clock. There was nothing we could do for him. One day he simply woke up and I was immediately called. When I entered his room I found a very depressed young man; he questioned why he had awakened. He explained to me that he had wanted to be a race car driver all his life, but his father had forbidden any such waste of his life with an occupation so horribly dangerous. He so desperately wanted to be a race car driver that he could not devote himself to any other occupation. He became more and more depressed, began to drink, and was wasting his life. One evening he dreamed that he was racing a car; he could see the car and all the gauges, as well as the activity when he went into the pit. He could feel the way it felt to drive, and he eventually won the race. He was handed a large trophy and received a kiss from a beautiful girl. Then he went home to a gorgeous apartment and got cleaned up for a party. His apartment had dozens of trophies scattered throughout the living room and bedroom. When he picked up a trophy, he could relive the excitement of the race; he just automatically knew about all the races he had won and what a wonderful life he had been living. He could clearly remember living this life, *all* of this life since childhood. Then one evening an unexpected visitor arrived. The man told him he could keep this life if he would help one other person find his dreams the way he found his. He didn't know what the man was talking about, but he quickly agreed and ushered him out the door, assuming he had just been visited by a lunatic. He had worked hard to achieve his deepest desires to race, and anybody else that wanted to achieve his goals could just work as hard as he had. There was nothing he could do to help somebody achieve his ambitious targets in life. He said he had no idea what the guy was talking about and then he told me with that thought, he woke up. The boy was trying to figure out if our conversation was a dream because he did not want us to be real and his racing life to be the dream. He was my first patient with this dream coma condition. I did not do a very good job with him. I had no idea what I was dealing with at the time, but even if I had, I don't know if I could have helped him. I arranged for him to see a psychiatrist right here at the hospital, but he was never able to keep even the first appointment. Two days after we spoke, his nurse went into a coma, right in his room, and he was right back in a coma. It was different from the first time. I could tell he was dreaming, but this time his lips were sucked in, just as you have seen in those rooms down the hallway. He was in a state of animation; his body did not need nourishment of any kind, nor did he expel any waste materials. He was very cold to the touch, extremely rigid, but not dead. It appeared that he had been frozen. A test showed his brain activity to be normal. We were all at a loss as to what to do with him, and his parents were frantic. He was not dead, but I was certain that he would never be returning again to this life.

When the nurse finally woke up, I had a little advance insight and began with the burning question as to why she had become a nurse. I felt a little small talk would put her at ease, and she just might tell me what I needed to know. She told me that since age 2 she had aspired to become a prima ballerina, but by age 8 it was obvious that her ankles were overly weak and she would never be able to dance for anything other than pleasure, and by age forty, she would have to give up anything that caused her ankles to twist and turn. Her parents talked her into a nursing career. Even though she had to stand on her feet most of the time, in the beginning years, there would come a time when she could do private duty nursing where she would be able to sit down a lot of the time. Having lost her dream, nursing was as good an occupation as any other.

She was the nurse for the boy who had been in a coma. He had talked her into dreaming about herself as a prima ballerina and told her she could be as good as she wanted to be when she was dreaming. She and the boy had laughed about it together. Then he convinced her to close her eyes and picture herself on the stage, in complete control, as the prima ballerina, and she dropped straight into a coma. I asked her what brought her out of the coma, and she knew at precisely what moment she had returned and why. A very strange man had stopped by her dressing room one evening and explained to her that she could only remain a ballerina if she helped one other person find his dream, and then she woke up. She explained that her life was so real, and so wonderful, that she was horrified when she awoke and realized that she was really a nurse and not a ballerina.

Her next remark frightened me so badly that I knew perfectly well that my suspicions must be correct.

"What made you decide to become a doctor?"

"I have to admit that I could not get out of her room quickly enough. In fact, I practically ran. I left orders that anybody who went into her room was to wear ear phones with music blasting in their ears. They were not to listen to her, read anything she wrote down, or speak to her. "Get in" and "get out" were strict orders. Absolutely no visitors were permitted, and a guard was placed at her doorway to make sure that no friends tried to slip into the room, feeling sorry for her isolation. I was not ready to explain myself to the nursing staff, but just asked them to follow my orders precisely as the situation was extremely critical.

When I got to my office, two of my colleagues were waiting to inform me about patients of theirs who were in comas, and we began to compare notes. Ridiculous as it may sound, we all three believed from the very beginning that these comas were somehow self-induced. I explained how I believed that the devil had devised a new method of acquiring souls. He has always been able to get the bad people, but he wanted the good ones also, and had come up with an ingenious way to obtain them with little effort on his part. They would remain alive, but would be in hell under his control forever. One colleague found my notion quite curious, although not believable, but the other was willing to accept the possibility. Explaining myself, I told them that I believed these people to be so engrossed in living their dreams that they were easy victims when the devil arrived to give them all they had ever wanted. Asleep they are exactly who they have wanted to be all their lives, especially if their real life is totally unsatisfying. When he comes to them in the form of a person and threatens to take away their new life unless they bring him a new person to whom he can give a better life, they don't really feel threatened, but feel that they must try to make another person happy if it would secure their own present life. They don't realize they are living a dream until they wake up and remember the "good life" they are living and desperately want to go back. I also do not think anybody realizes that he is talking directly to the devil.

After they go into these states of animation, where we are not able to help them, we have no way to communicate with them to convince them to fight for their very lives and souls. I don't think they get to keep their dream lives very long and I'll show you why." Once again, Dr. Overman took her arm and without another word he led her down the hallway to huge double doors. When he opened the doors the room was lighted about like twilight, but even in the dimness she could see the faces of the people nearest to her. Each had some kind of a horrible scream frozen on their face that made her cry out in horror. Mary grabbed her mouth as though she might awaken somebody. Tears fell from her eyes again, and she could only look at Dr. Overman, but she could not talk.

"Mary, we decided to bring every coma victim to this building when they wake, explain what we think is going on, and show them their destiny. We have to immediately cover their mouths and handcuff them behind their backs in order to get them here safely, and without them trying to send someone else to their ruination. Hopefully, we can win back some of the souls when they are instructed to come back and recruit somebody else."

Mary put up her hand to stop him for a moment. "You are saying that people who never achieved their dreams in real life are going into comas where they are everything they ever wanted to be, but the devil makes them come back for another person under threat of taking away their dream life. Is that correct?"

"That is exactly correct, and our worst fear is that word of this will get out to the public before we are able to help these people, as well as future victims, and can you imagine what a joke it would become? Doctors believe the devil is alive and well and giving people their lifelong dreams, and that is what doctors are using as an excuse for not treating coma patients, simply because they have no clue what is wrong with them. The devil is counting on nobody believing what is happening because that is the easiest way to keep them coming to him. Every day we have to move people from the smaller rooms into this room because they seem to be past our helping them. When the sucked in lips go into a horrific scream, we know they are gone for good. They are not dead, but they can't come back. We continue to try to find some way to bring the dreamers back before the scream appears on their face. I have to tell you, though, we just can't seem to work fast enough. I'm showing you all this in the hopes that you will be able to talk with your grandmother and gain some information for us that may be helpful. Your grandmother has been awake three times and you have always been with her. It's a long shot, but you are the first relative that seems to be *so* close, that your very closeness keeps her coming back. This is her fourth coma;

these other victims all had one dream coma before going back permanently. I don't know how she is getting back into the coma without having brought anybody else, and we can't find any evidence that ties her into any of our other victims. We have fairly clear records to indicate who brought whom into the dream coma world, and in none of these cases can I find any evidence that your grandmother is involved. Every room where we keep a coma victim, we also keep a 24-hour tape running, so we have been able to determine at least how the comas occur and who causes one to whom. Please help us. What does she say to you? She always has her hand covering her mouth and looks as if she is whispering."

"Every time she has recovered, she tells me these wild stories about her dreams, just as though they were real. I just let her ramble because I thought she was having some kind of breakdown and the stories did not seem, in any way, to be dangerous. And yes, she asked me each time what I wanted most out of my life, and each time I have told her the same thing; I have everything I could desire. I have a wonderful grandmother to love me and take care of me, my job makes me so happy that I cannot imagine doing anything else with my life, and the only thing I'm missing is my cat, who died last month. I've been waiting for her to get well so we can go together to get a new kitten. She has never been happy with my answers and insists that I must have dreamed of being something special when I was a little girl and I should think very hard about it and let her know. It is very important to her that she know what it is that I desire more than anything else in the world. Does that help you at all? Maybe the devil can't find a way to deal with happy, satisfied people, and if she can get me to surrender to him, then he will know how to get others like me to give in to his horrible schemes."

"Thank you Mary, for your understanding and your kindness in helping us. You can imagine that this is becoming an epidemic. We have eight floors in this building, and it houses hundreds of people. There are many countries around the world that are beginning to have dream coma epidemics as well, and we will not be able to keep it a secret much longer. The public will be petrified when they find out that just going to sleep can trigger a coma. They will fear that their children will desire a future so badly that they will fall into a coma. Single parents will panic at the thought of going to sleep and leaving their children. People will stop trusting others and will stop having conversations about their achievements and what they wish to attain in the future. We've got to find some answers soon, and right now you are our only hope. It's not much of a connection, but it is the only one we have to the other side."

"Dr. Overman, I don't know how much help I'll be, but I will stay by my grandmother's side, and when she wakes up, I'll do everything in my power to convince her to stay with us and to tell us everything she knows."

Mary waited another 3 weeks before her grandmother woke up, and when she did, she was very unpleasant. She knew all about Mary's talk with Dr. Overman and how they were planning to take away her life as a famous singer. She ranted and raved about how she had given up her dreams as a young girl, gotten married and raised five children because that was what women were supposed to do and did not run off to New

York like some "hussy," as her mother had called her when she expressed her desire to be an entertainer. When Mary Scott's parents died, Doris had taken her daughter's child into her own home and raised her as her own child, giving her all the love and attention she had given her own children. Now, when she finally had a chance to realize her dream of becoming a singing sensation, and she was quite a hit, Mary wanted to take it all away.

"Gramma, you are already a singing sensation at church, and you have brought such happiness into the lives of so many over the years. How can you say you are not a success?"

"I wanted to be a rich and famous singer and travel and be in shows and on the stage. Can't you understand that? If you really love me, you'll come with me so I can stay."

"In your dream coma, in your successful, famous life, do you know what day it is each day?"

"I don't know what you mean."

"Oh, yes you do! Now answer me. Do you know when it is Monday or Tuesday, or Sunday, so you can go to church? You have rarely missed a day of church in your entire life. Do you know what day it is or not?"

"Who cares, but no, I don't."

"That is because the devil is controlling your artificial success while you dream and he will not let you know what day it is because he does not *want* you to care. If you know it is Sunday, you might think of church, or Tuesday being circle time, or maybe Wednesday prayer meeting. If you start thinking about church, you will think about God, and he won't be able to hold you. Isn't that right?"

"Leave me alone. I'm tired."

"You're not the least bit tired. Dr. Overman is on his way; and we are going for a little ride, and you are going to see just where you are headed."

Mary began pulling her grandmother out of the bed and was surprised by the force with which she resisted. Dr. Overman arrived with the wheelchair and it took the strength of both of them, plus tying her into the chair with belts and cords, before they were ready to take her to the Dream Coma Center. They went to the first group who were just dreaming with their lips sucked in, and Dr. Overman explained their state of suspension. Then he rolled her into the large room where all appeared to have crossed over into Hell and were screaming. Doris covered her face with her hands and cried out her heart. She recognized the first man in the room because he had been her first friend in her dream coma. They did a duet together and were a perfect couple in harmony without any practice. One night he simply vanished and nobody seemed to know where he had gone. Now she knew. Seeing John Freeman in Hell did more to convince Doris of the seriousness of the matter than anything else.

"Doc, have you got a cross on you?" said Doris.

He certainly did have one, and had been carrying one every day for the past couple of years since this craziness started. Mary had a rather large cross around her neck that she had been wearing since her grandmother's first coma. She would hold onto it and pray for her sweet grandmother to return to her.

She took it off and gave it to Dr. Overman. Doris asked the doctor to roll her over to her friend so she could watch him as the cross was laid on his chest. John's face relaxed, and he died. Dr. Overman felt his pulse and noted that his arm was no longer freezing. He listened to his heart, and the man was certainly dead. He grabbed Doris' cheeks, and kissed her on the nose, and ran from the room, yelling back over his shoulder for Mary to get her grandmother back to her room.

Dr. Overman ran straight to the hospital Chapel, told the Chaplain to get every cross he had, every Bible available, and to follow him. He was on the phone to other doctors working the dream coma patients and explained what they were about to do. He told them to bring as many crosses and as much help as they could find.

"We are going to kill them all. Apparently, the only way the devil could get the souls of decent people, Christian people, was to keep them alive in a frozen state. If they die, they then have a chance to get out of Hell and into Heaven."

They ran back to the Dream Coma Center and for the next few hours, joined by doctors and nurses bringing crosses and Bibles, they killed the damned, in one room after another. Going from hammock to hammock they released the screaming undead, which had been tricked into Hell. Now as they died they could go to Heaven and be judged by God. When they had finished, he explained to the Chaplain his fears that the others were still in the middle of their dreams. He did not feel that they were dead, but just dreaming, and wondered out loud what damage they might do if they used the crosses and the word of God. The Chaplain explained that they could do no further damage than had already been done, and if there was any way in the world to save them, it was their obligation to try. They began with the last victim who had arrived only that morning. Laying the cross on the woman's chest and reading from the Bible, the Chaplain was thrilled to see her slowly open her eyes and release her clenched lips. He smiled at her and she returned the smile. He gave Dr. Overman the high sign and everybody began to work on releasing the victims. As the victims awoke, they were in a state of confusion about where they were or why, but nobody spoke a word. They were confused to awaken to so many people around them. There were so many people in gowns, getting out of hammocks, and then there were others who all seemed to be intent on awakening everyone. Somehow, the massive confusion seemed to explain to them the horror of where they had really been, and they began to seek each other out and hold hands and cry. There were dozens of nurses and doctors helping to get the victims awake, and they began to take them outside into the sunlight. Families had to be called, explanations had to be made, countries had to be alerted, but nothing was more important right now that getting people to wake up. They were all holding on to their crosses for dear life.

Dr. Overman knew that the entire world would have to hear what had happened and how the dream coma patients were saved. It would be one of those stories where the listeners did not have the capacity to take it all in; the horror of such a thing being even barely possible could not be digested by rational people. However, should one of their loved ones fall into a coma, they would remember, and they would lay a cross on their chest and open the Bible and begin to read. And that is when they would believe.

In all the confusion and the hard work to save lives, Dr. Overman had completely forgotten about Mary Scott and her grandmother. He ran as fast as he could to Doris' room and just fell to his knees crying when he entered. Mary had given up her cross, and it had cost her not only her own life…but that of her grandmother. They were both huddled in a corner with their arms around each other and the horrible scream etched on both their faces. He knelt down and prayed for both of their souls before laying the cross on each of them to release them from Hell and into the death they deserved with the God they had served and loved all their lives.

As Dr. Overman sat there completely overcome by the unbelievable events of the day, a man appeared in the doorway and he began to laugh and laugh. His laughter grew louder until it pierced the eardrums and caused everybody to come running to quiet the disturbance. "I'll be back for you," he said. Then he vanished. The doctor held the cross close to his chest and vowed he would always be ready to fight.

BUDDIES

Raymond thought about his five buddies—the ones that he was growing up with—and decided that now that they were all in the seventh grade, they were old enough to make a very important decision about their lives. He told them the next day that they had to discuss something important and that it had to be kept a secret, because nobody else needed to know their business. They all quickly agreed and planned to meet at Raymond's house directly after school to discuss his idea. They always said they were *laying the groundwork* as their code words for making plans because one of their dad's had said that when planning for their vacation and it sounded so mysterious and cool, that they immediately stole the saying for their own.

After school, they went to Raymond's house, grabbed cookies and drinks, and went straight into groundwork mode. None of them knew what Raymond had in mind, but they knew it would be good. Raymond was the nerd, geek, brains of the group, and when he said they needed to do something, they knew he was serious.

"All right, listen up men." They always referred to each other as *men* when discussions were to be serious. Any other time they would have used all kinds of insulting terms like "pig breath" and such. Raymond asked if they were aware of the boy who got snatched by some goon right in front of his school, waiting on his mom to pick him up. They all nodded. Then he asked if they knew about the boy who was snatched just down the road when he was riding his bike to the store. They all spoke at the same time. None of them knew anything about it and asked who it was and why Raymond knew and they did not. Raymond asked them if they had been kept away from the news recently, and they all agreed that they had and that their parents had been giving lame excuses for why they did not want any evening news. The boys had been in the habit of watching a little local news each evening and then discussing how they would have handled the situation, but only Raymond knew about this kidnapping and they knew exactly how he knew. Raymond was an avid radio fan. When his parents hid newspapers or tried to distract him from the local news, he just went to his room and listened to the radio and got the scoop. It was kind of old fashioned, but it got the job done.

Parents always try to protect their children from the horrors of life when it is just around the corner. They never realize that they do more harm by keeping secrets that the children will discover one way or another. The parents of the "buddies" thought it was cute the way the boys watched the news and talked about what they would have done and how easily they would have solved a problem or a crime. As long as it did not touch home, it was all in fun, but when a kidnapping happened in the neighborhood, it was no longer funny.

"Do you all remember the red-headed guy, a teenager, who gave us a five-dollar bill at the store and told us to get cookies and drinks? We could not believe that a teenager would be so nice and to guys he did not even know. Remember what he said when we asked him why?"

Bill popped up and said, "I will never forget it for the rest of my life. He said, "Do a good deed every day for absolutely no other reason than you will make somebody happy." I never heard anybody say anything better than that, even at church. You are not going to tell us that he was the kid that got snatched are you?"

"Yes, I am. And they know it was a kidnapping because they found his bike and it had blood on it. The police have no idea who took him."

Dan said to Raymond, "And what are we going to do about it?"

"We can't do anything to help him, but we can sure do something to keep ourselves safe, and here is what we are going to do. Nobody will let us carry weapons and only one of us would be any good at using them anyway, and that is Slugger. Am I right guys?" All heads nodded yes. "So, I'm saying we need to stick together all the time and we need to learn to use the one good weapon we all have and that is our teeth." Everybody said "What??" at the same time, and then belly laughed for a few minutes. When they had wiped their eyes and settled down, Raymond grabbed slugger's arm and bit down hard, causing him to scream and try to pull away, but he did not hit Raymond, who let go immediately. "Now, do you see what happened? Slugger did not hit at me, but tried to pull away and so would any kidnapper who was being bitten by a bunch of guys. He would be doing his best to get away safely while we were taking pieces out of him. We have to practice hard and build up our nerve to bite and hang on for dear life so we can do as much damage as possible."

"And suppose we do all this hard work and practicing and never have to attack anybody, said Rob."

Clifford just looked at him as though looking at the dumbest dog on the planet and said, "Look numb nuts, what we learn now could end up saving us fifty years from now. You never waste your time when you learn to do something to keep yourself safe. At school we learn how to get out of a house on fire. Suppose you are never in a fire. Was it a waste of time to learn about it? You can really be a bonehead when you want to, you know?"

"Yeah, yeah. So, what do we do and when do we start?"

Raymond said that he felt Slugger should be in charge of the whole plan to stick together, practicing attacking with just a couple guys, a few guys, and all the guys. They had to know their strategy before anything ever happened. Slugger accepted the responsibility and began to lay out ideas. The main thing was for them to never be alone going to school or coming home. They all lived within a few houses of each other, and the last two could easily watch each other get inside the door.

The buddies—Raymond, Bill, Dan, Clifford, Slugger and Rob—protected each other from that day forward. When one guy was sick, the others checked on him during the day by calling him and accusing him of being a faker. If one or two were gone on vacations, the others took care to be on the watch out for one another.

This sacred attention to one another took on a strange momentum, all its own, as they became teenagers. Each boy took a different path in life; sports, computers, dance, and all the oddball interests that teenagers develop as they mature. If one wanted to go to a ballgame at night, then they all went whether or not they had any interest in the game. Only two of them liked to go to the school dances, but they all went, with or without dates. Nobody ever went on a date alone, but would double date or triple date. The parents of the girls they dated thought they were just the best young men ever because they went in groups and it was better protection for their daughters.

After graduation, Raymond went to the local university, Slugger joined the police force, Bill and Dan both wanted to be firemen, Clifford worked in his dad's fence-building business, and Rob began to train as a landscaper. They could not get out of the habit of taking care of each other, so they decided to rent a big house for all of them to share. It was agreed that they would stay there until each married off to somebody. This idea evoked a great deal of teasing and carrying on about the girls they dated. It was agreed that the house was their sanctuary and no girls were ever to be allowed inside. It was the big boys' clubhouse, and it was a wonderful life for about the first week. Then they all realized that their moms were not fixing their dinners anymore and had to have a meeting to lay the groundwork about cooking. Their decision was superb. They decided to actually take courses in cooking. Rob was naturally concerned that he would go to all this trouble to learn to cook, then get married and never have to use his skills. That remark caused such a racket of belly laughs and jabs about his ugly self and who in tarnation would marry him and jibes that he would be cooking for himself for the next sixty years, that they could barely speak for rolling over the couch and chairs and on the floor. Rob had been through this teasing crap with these guys all his life, and it just rolled off his back like water off a duck's back.

"Yeah, yeah. Fine, I'll learn to cook. Damn bunch of idiots to have to live with anyway!"

The boys were surprised that they were enjoying the cooking classes and once they had the basics down, took another class on meats, then vegetables, and moved on into breads and desserts. Truth be told, they were fighting over who was going to get to cook in the evenings. They tried to share the duties, but could never agree, so they decided to split up the evenings. According to their own working schedules, they would write in their names when they would be in complete charge of the evening meal. That meant they would shop for the food and cook the meal. It was a brilliant plan and worked beautifully, and then Raymond came up with another brainstorm.

"Guys, I think we should have one night a month when one of us plans a special dinner, with a dress code, and an activity to go with the splendid meal. We need to learn to have a little class, in preparation of impressing the right woman so she will agree to marriage."

As ideas go it was a little corny, but they did not want to become know-nothing, do-nothing, couch potatoes, and it was ever so much fun when their peers at work showed amazement at their constant ingenuity. In some ways, they were setting the example for the new modern male of today. Women wanted equality, so why couldn't men have equality and not be embarrassed to learn many of the tasks traditionally assigned to women?

They discussed it for over an hour before they finally agreed on the rules. No women or family would be invited to the special meals *inside* their house. The activity had to be something entertaining and new, not just a movie or some board game or charades. The activity should be something that none of them had ever done before in order for them to experience something new. Since there were six of them, that meant they would only have the duty twice a year and that seemed like something they could handle financially and mentally, and so *the groundwork had been laid.*

Bill, a fireman, had drawn the first evening, and he was quite pleased because there was something he wanted to do and he was afraid the guys would think him a moron if he just brought it up any other time. Now, he was in charge of an activity, and nobody was going to complain for fear that their own activity would get criticized.

Bill's evening arrived. His dress code was tee-shirts and jeans. Everybody was relieved and wondered what in the world he had planned. He used their indoor barbecue to cook the pork chops to a perfect brown but just as tender and juicy as any expert chef could achieve. With the chops he had rice and gravy and a hot applesauce with cinnamon. He served a delicious white wine and received nothing but praise. When everybody had finished eating, he told them that the activity would take place first and then the dessert would be served. Everybody went into the living room, and he handed each one a box.

"So, open them already," he said. The boys opened their boxes to find rope ladders inside. When their question mark faces looked up at him he grinned.

"Fire escape ladders are what they are boys, and with Dan's help, we will show you how to set them up and use them should the occasion ever arise." The guys were surprised and quite pleased that he had thought of such a thing for their safety. There was a front door and no other means of escape from this big old house. All the bedrooms were upstairs, and if this old tinderbox caught on fire, they would never be able to get out alive. They praised him greatly, learned how to use them, and then actually practiced escaping. They all agreed that they would meet under the oak tree in the front yard so nobody would be getting killed trying to save somebody that was already out of the house. After everybody was satisfied that they knew what to do in case of an emergency, they went back inside for dessert and coffee. The guys were secretly glad to learn the escape plan and to have the ladder. They knew that when they had a family, it would be a welcome relief to be prepared to keep their family safe. A happy bunch of men went to their own spaces to watch TV, listen to music, work on the computer, make phone calls, or whatever they wanted to do, in their own rooms with their own time.

When the next special night came it belonged to Slugger, and he attacked the evening just as he did everything else: directly, head-on, and without any finesse. The dress code was that there *was* no dress code. His meal would be steaks, baked potatoes with all the trimmings, and green beans. His desert would be a lemon meringue pie. There was a hearty red wine and a special coffee and liquor with the pie. The compliments were constant all around. Everybody who still had a dinner to plan swore they could never top the two dinners they had already enjoyed. Slugger and Bill agreed, and they all had a good laugh.

Slugger told them all to go into the living room for the activity. Five excited men dashed for the best spots in the living room, which included one overstuffed couch and two extremely manly leather chairs. They had spared no expense on their décor, all of which had been purchased in thrift shops, and all of which had seen its better days. Slugger opened the coat closet, brought out a box and went around handing each one of his friends a stun gun. "Boys, I'm going to show you how to use them, and I want you to keep them with you at all times. The boys spent the next couple of hours learning how to use the stun guns to ward off an attacker and a couple of them even volunteered to be the victim and get shot; they were able to attest to the fact that it would take down a big man.

Thus far the special dinners were a raving success!

When it was Rob's turn, he said the dress code would be slacks and Hawaiian shirts. Nobody smelled anything cooking, so they were highly suspicious about Rob's plan. As it turned out, he was taking them to a Luau and he was one of the cooks. The activity was none other than true Hawaiian entertainment. Since Rob was helping do the cooking for over 200 people, he said his guests got in for free. Leave it to Rob to come up with a plan that would not cost him a cent. He did, however, take them all in a limo so that none of them would have to drive home intoxicated, and they gave him great praise for his planning. Knowing Rob, he just wanted to show off with the limo and used the drinking line as an excuse.

When Clifford's turn came, he did a backyard barbecue and invited every guy's dad, which brought a tear to many an eye. What a surprise! The activity was horseshoes, and everyone had a great time. The dads complimented their sons on their desire to learn to cook and take care of themselves. This conduct would never have been accepted in their day, and that left a lot of old men hungry when their wives either left or died. The sons all laughed and suggested that their dads hang on to their moms.

Dan had to think long and hard, not to one-up anybody, but just to come close to his evening being a success. He did not want to be known as the worst planner of all time, and the guys would raze him mercilessly if he flopped. He finally decided on taking his buds to a sports bar for the biggest game of the year, but then he was not cooking, so that would be a cop-out. No, he could not do that! Then it hit him. The dinner would be at his mom's home with just the moms. They had done something with the fathers. Now he would do a meal with just the moms. He fixed the simple meal of hamburgers, homemade potato chips, coleslaw, and fresh lemonade. Dan was extremely self-conscious when planning the meal. It was important to him that he not outdo any of the moms with his cooking. For the activity they would take pictures for all the moms, Raymond would print them off right then and there, and the frames would be ready and waiting. Ah, what a tearjerker night that would be. The dress code would have to be dress shirts and slacks for the pictures. He pitied poor Raymond for being last, but little did he know that the evening he planned was about to set the stage for Raymond's.

At 6 pm they were all sitting around the table passing this and that when the front and back doors both burst open at the same time and three men came rushing in with guns telling everybody to get up and get their faces against the wall. Each boy grabbed his mother to protect her, but the men with guns said the women were to go to the kitchen with the guy that came in the back door. It was lunacy all around when the boys' reflexes kicked in and they jumped on the guys and bit the ever loving hell out of them. Slugger was biting and shooting all at the same time. He always wore a gun at the ankle, and he took one guy down in seconds. The biters held on for dear life, and the mothers ran for the bedroom and the phone. Raymond took a bullet in the arm, but it went straight through. He grabbed his stun gun off his belt and shot the guy in the face; down he went. The fight lasted no more than a few minutes, but the room looked like fifty guys had come through on horses. Slugger slammed them all up against the wall and demanded to know what the hell they were after. They said they were after the stolen drug money. He looked around the room and there was nothing but blank faces looking back at him. He turned back to the guy and asked, "Who the hell here has stolen any drug money, what is the name of the person you are looking for." He nearly fainted on the spot when the guy pointed and said **him!** Slugger slowly turned and was looking directly into the face of Rob. Slugger just said they were crazy and had Rob confused with some guy who just looked like him and they were all three going off to jail. The police arrived a few minutes later and hauled them off.

Nobody said a word to Rob while they pacified the moms, cleaned up the house and drove home. As soon as they were inside the door, Slugger grabbed Rob by the front of the shirt and threw him clear across the room. When Rob finally caught his breath, he explained what happened. He had been at an ice cream parlor, just sitting at a table and looking out the window at people passing by. He could see them, but the way he was seated, they really could not see him watching them. He saw a guy walk by and place a backpack into the city trash can, and knowing this was an odd occurrence, he retrieved the backpack, got into his car, and left. Somebody must have been watching to see that the pack was picked up by the right person, and seeing him take it; they must have gotten his tag number, found him, and followed him to get the money back. He checked the bag at a stop light, and seeing that he had acquired a fortune, decided to pass the money along just like that teenager long ago. He wanted to do it in memory of him. He had spent the rest of the day passing out some of the money. He did not give too much to each recipient so as to not alert anybody that anything was wrong. He had given money to women who looked too poor to buy good food, slipped money in the box at church, gone to the hospital and paid a couple of bills for old guys who could not pay their own bills. Slugger decided they needed to just kill Rob as he was just too damn dumb to live. That broke the tension, and they all just shook their heads at his ignorance. Rob went and got the backpack, and the guys could not believe the stacks of money. They discussed giving it back, but decided they would die anyway. They sat up for hours just trying to find a way to stay alive. Drug dealers do just one thing with thieves who take their money: kill them!

Slugger called some of his cop friends and asked them to do a little off-duty body guard job. They stayed with Rob for two days while the others tried to find a way to stay alive. The three that tried to kill them were in jail without bond because they tried to kill a cop. They had no idea that Slugger was a cop, or they would have waited for Rob to be alone before roughing him up, getting their money, and then killing him. An informant told Slugger that one of the guys in prison, a guy named Sammy, was the one who dropped the money and he was trying to get it back before his boss killed him, so, the only person who knew that somebody else got the money was him and one of his guys who was on lookout duty to be sure that the right people picked up the dough. Nobody he knew had ever actually laid eyes on the big boss because money was always passed this way for safety: keep those in charge secret. This routine had been working for years and kept people out of jail by changing the drop each time. It was just their word against Rob's that the money was stolen. How would the boss feel about it if the dealer was the one who kept the money for himself and just blamed it on a citizen who happened to be in the wrong place at the wrong time?

Slugger worked the streets, knew many of the sleaze bags that worked the drug racket, and stayed one step ahead of the law. He made sure that the word got out on the streets that a drug dealer had kept money that was supposed to be paid up-the-line and accused some little dork at the ice cream shop in order to keep the loot and get the kid killed. He said Sammy was bragging about it in prison, and said that he would probably get a couple of years for roughing up a family party, but nobody got killed or anything, and when he got out he would have nearly a million bucks to take him away to party land. He was tired of working the streets while some guy got rich but never got his hands dirty. That information was whispered all over the streets and right on up the chain. All three idiots were all of a sudden receiving the best attorney representation imaginable; they got off with probation and turned up dead two days after their release.

Raymond decided he would give his party and the dress code would be black. He intended to set the mood to correspond to the nightmare situation in which they found themselves. Black shirts, pants, socks, and shoes were the order of the evening. The table cloth was black; napkins black, candles were black and the cloud that hung over the room was black. The meal was the meal of the mafia: spaghetti, loaves of French bread and red wine. After the meal was quietly eaten, they moved to the living room for what would probably be a gloomy conversation.

"Gentlemen, we need to *lay the groundwork* for finding this big boss in the drug ring, getting rid of him and hopefully stay alive ourselves, and try to clean up this town a little. Nobody is ever again going to break into one of our homes and scare our families half to death. I consider each of you my family, and the fact that some of us damn near died during the battle will keep me awake nights. Now I know we are just a bunch of guys, but I think we have the collective talents and wits to pull this thing off. What do you say?"

"Are you out of your freaking mind?" said Rob. "It's my damn fault all this happened in the first place, and I'm not going to take any more chances with my life or any of yours. We are lucky as hell that Slugger was able to find a way to keep that drug boss off my back or I would not be sitting here right now."

"I wasn't serious guys." A sigh of relief was felt by everybody. "We know absolutely nothing about drug rings or drug dealers. Whoever this powerful guy is who heads this city's drug business would have us all killed just as soon as he got wind of our snooping around. As I see it, all we can do is to keep our mouths shut, not spend very much at any given time and never let anybody know our secret."

"You guys have failed to realize something very important," said Slugger. First of all, I'm a cop and I have personally broken a few laws and would be kicked off the force if anybody finds out. All of you know we have drug money in the house and that is a law breaker. This is extremely serious guys."

"Now wait just a minute," said Clifford. You have one hell of a lot of money in that backpack, don't you Rob?"

"Yeah, so?"

"Just how much do you have left, or do you even know?"

"No, I don't know."

"All right, go get it and let's count it."

Rob went off to his room to get the money. When he brought it back he placed it on the table for the guys to count while he went to the kitchen to fix coffee. There was over $900,000 still in the backpack. It needed to be spent, and they had to decide right now how to spend it so that no eyebrows would be raised. First they decided on home alert safety for each of their parents with the monthly fees paid for the next five years. That was something a son could do without raising any suspicions even from the parents. They decided that they were all so tired that they needed to go to bed and would continue the conversation tomorrow evening after supper when they had given it some thought during the day. The whole fiasco had taken a toll on everybody and the guys went directly to bed without even taking showers, brushing teeth, watching the news or doing anything. Just as Slugger closed his eyes his brain clicked in and he remembered that not everybody had the coffee and all he could say to himself was *please let me be wrong.*

At 2 A.M. a shadow crept into each room and carried out the fire escape ladders, then slipped down the stairs spilling gasoline as it went. When reaching the front door the downstairs was saturated with gas. The match was lit, flicked onto the gas, and the shadow stepped outside with the backpack, vanishing into the night.

THE VOLUNTEERS

A beautiful planet is located many light years away, past Orion's Belt, and is simply called *Star*. The land masses are divided into eight large sectors, very much as the Earth is divided into countries. These sectors are numbered, and those who live in each have been charged, since the beginning of its time, with the responsibility of watching over particular areas on Earth. The leaders in each sector decide when to intervene in the country for which they are responsible, just as they have always done, beginning when humans were created. Sometimes the Star leaders feel it is best to wait and watch, and other times they feel it is best to interfere. For the future betterment of the Earth, they have created erupting volcanoes, earthquakes, tornadoes, tsunamis, and plagues to control an explosion of the population or the destructive behaviors of the residents.

In ancient times they came to Earth and interacted with the inhabitants in exchange for their digging for the minerals needed on Star. Earthlings were taught the secrets of how to build massive caverns-inside mountains-to house thousands of people for protection from attack, unlock the secret to building huge, exquisitely detailed pyramids, and write down the languages they spoke. They also taught them to build landing strips for the spaceships from Star, and how to temporarily capture gravity in order to raise massive stones for walls and religious centers and move them where needed without effort. Their visitations were recorded throughout the histories of these countries, and pictures of the visitors from Star were captured on the walls of caves in rudimentary images. Even today, many tribes still celebrate when the gods from Star came to Earth, in the same manner passed down from generation to generation.

The children of Star are called *Starlings* until they reach the age of two hundred. They then become adults and are referred to as *Starians*, a name that remains until they are one thousand. At that time they become known as *Pleasures* and are allowed to travel to other sectors, take any of the flights to Earth to observe the earthlings, and become advisors to the leadership of Star. Most remain *Pleasures* for about five hundred years, until their death when they are transformed into stars in the night sky, remaining so until they are reborn on Star and begin life over as a *Starling*. The leaders in each sector are called *The Couple*, and they are the ones who address whether or not there is a need to intervene with life on Earth.

The Star planet is covered in rich vegetation with berries, fruits, and nuts growing everywhere. Birds of countless numbers inhabit the trees, and the population is controlled by capturing limited numbers for meals. The waters are filled with great varieties of fish, and there is no limit to the number caught for consumption. Because there is no money on Star, the bird capturers and the fishermen trade their catches for things they need. No predators, of any kind, roam the forests, making a walk through various areas quite pleasant and never dangerous. Likewise, one may swim in the waters without fear of any danger. There is no wealth or poverty on Star because families share their belongings with one another and items are passed from generation to generation. Starians remain within their sector throughout their lives, until they become a *Pleasure*, when they are allowed to travel outside their designated sector. Since family members always remain within either their home or that of their companion, possessions never leave the families. There is no need for money, just a talent for trading.

The men and women of Star select their companion around the age of three hundred, having finished their studies and become adults selecting their lifetime vocation. Looking for a mate on Star is a very serious business, as each must make a full and complete confession to the other as to his/her desires for life, wishes to have or not have children, and all the other life commitments. Once a pair makes their agreements to belong to each other, they can never part. This solemn ceremony is attended only by the two people pledging their lives; no other person may ever know what they said to each other unless they wish to share the information. If they both agree not to have children, they are voluntarily sterilized. The only person who would know about this action would be the sterilizer.

There is a 300-year cycle in which a female *Starian* can become pregnant with a child. It is mandatory that parents give their full attention to a child during the 200 years it is in study and the 100 years of vocation selection and apprenticeship. Their constant dedication to this child assures that he/she becomes a worthy Star citizen. It concerns them greatly that earthlings reproduce at will and devote very little time to the education and vocation of each child. The Starians reason that this is the underlying cause of so much crime throughout the countries on Earth. It is a simple matter of neglect.

The Couple in Sector 8, known as Serena and Kern, are, by law, childless. The Couple are charged with dedicating their lives to the business of their sector and ensuring that it continues to run as smoothly as it did with the administration of all The Couples before them. They have the benefit of the advice of all the *Pleasures*, and when a particularly difficult decision has to be made, advisers can be brought together, from the various Sectors, to discuss the situation.

Serena and Kern had been studying the States of America, *their* area of responsibility, very closely in the last fifty years and were amazed that two quite different life choices were becoming prevalent but were quite at odds with each other. First, the scientific community was finally beginning to agree that man did not create, and could not possibly have created, the massive stone pyramid at Giza, or intricate caves chiseled completely out of a mountain. Man could not have sliced off the top of the mountain in Peru to accommodate the Nazca lines visible only from the air. All over the world could be found amazing feats of architecture: the 887 Moai of Easter Island that guarded the coast; Stonehenge, the giant, finely carved blocks at Puma Punku in the Bolivian highland; and a hundred more sites, plus many not yet discovered. Ancient man, with his elementary little tools, could not achieve these miraculous monuments. Archeologists and scientists have attempted to duplicate, physically and by computer program, many of the ancient accomplishments, without success, unless modern technology was used, thus proving that ancient man, without these devices, could not possibly have accomplished such massive buildings and intricate work. The Earth's scientific community is becoming aware that somebody, from somewhere, came to Earth and showed man *how* to build... helped him to build, and are telling the public about all their findings, thus making the public aware that the past was under scrutiny.

Some of the areas in question were being explored/and discussed before the public by means of the television and web sites on the computer, thus involving everybody who might have an interest, comment, or a desire to get involved in the exploration of information about his/her true origins and past civilizations.

The Mayan village with its amazing structures was home to men of genius. They devised a calendar that began before they even existed and stopped on December 21, 2012. Why? Numerous discussions were underway, trying to determine why they began their calendar at a date prior to their existence, and stopped the calendar far after they vanished. There is no record as to why they left, leaving many ancient UFO researchers declaring that they were aliens and simply went home. Pacal, the ruler of the Mayan city of Palenque in southern Mexico was placed into his sarcophagus, which was carved to portray him departing Earth in a spaceship. The sarcophagus was placed inside a pyramid called the Temple of Inscriptions. Who did the carving... and *why*?

There are massive walls where each rock was fused with the next in such a manner that not even a piece of paper could slide between them. This was not a feat that man could accomplish. How were they fused and who did the work? Could ancient man, with his limited abilities and tools, accomplish such feats? Modern man has not yet figured out how to fuse the rocks together without using modern technology. The scientific community involved the entire world, in their investigations, by showing these sites and accomplishments to every individual who wanted to follow the trails of investigation without ever leaving their homes. Could the discoveries help to prove that ancient aliens visited the Earth?

Many Earthlings believe that these aliens had to have a hand in changing the gene structure in man in order to turn him from a caveman into a modern, intelligent man virtually overnight, because there are drawings and sculptures everywhere indicating that Earth was visited in the past. The visitors were not just watching, but were working. Earthlings are trying to decipher the messages left behind in order to discover exactly who the visitors were, why they came, if they will return, and when. Obviously the aliens went to a lot of trouble to make sure that eventually modern man would begin to genuinely question the inscriptions and the written histories of the countries who recorded events, as well as they could, with the knowledge they had at the time. All this information has always been treated as myth, but when they are regarded as the truth of what actually took place, they take on a whole new meaning, and it is this knowledge that is opening the eyes and minds of Earthlings.

The Couple addressed the volunteers. "While many Earthlings are wrapped up in the attempt to understand the true history of Earth, there are countless people who are destroying the Earth and its inhabitants. The valuable forests are being cut down, without regard to the damage it will cause to the future of the Earth. There are those who grow and sell dangerous drugs to a great portion of the people throughout the world. Both of these groups have devastated two valuable resources: man and

Earth. However, Sector 8 is concerned about the drugs and the effect they are having on all humans world-wide. Each sector is planning to approach the problem in the countries that are their responsibility. The *Pleasures* have agreed to discuss the problem of the devastation of the forests and get back to the concerned sectors for their approval. We are focused only on the drug problem in the States of America and how we shall solve the usage that leads to addiction and criminal activities against those who are innocent victims.

The drug lords ship their wares to any country where they can enter without being caught. When the drugs get to the dealers, they in turn sell to the very people who are least able to resist being exploited. Young people get addicted, lose interest in everything and everybody, and destroy what future they might have had. Women become pregnant with children they cannot raise properly, live off the country's welfare system and use whatever income they receive to continue to buy drugs. They become pregnant again and again, and the children grow up to be like their parents: irresponsible and addicted to drugs. The world is becoming overrun with these dangerous, ignorant people."

The Couple addressed the *Starlings* as Saviors of America. "We are not responsible for the entire Earth, only the states of America, our area of responsibility. Your job will be to sterilize each and every drug addict, and his/her children, in order to prevent reproduction of these potentially harmful individuals. Hopefully, they will die off and they will not have any progeny to follow in their footsteps, and you will help curb some of the crime committed by the drug addicts. We could just wipe out entire communities, but this solution would kill off the few children who might become useful citizens.

You will each be given a star that will appear on the underside of the web area between your thumb and pointer finger. Unless you hold your hand up and spread your fingers, it cannot be seen. This star must touch the person, as you think *sterilize,* in order to be effective. You will each be responsible for sterilizing as many drug addicts as you can possibly touch. Your 'birth' will take place after you have slept for nine months. The second you are born, touch the mother to be sure you are the last child she ever bears. You will be born with most of your powers intact, such as your ability to read minds, project the futures of individuals, and record everything you see, hear, and read. However, you will not be strong and will have no ability to kill anyone with your mind. Never let any human realize your intelligence. Make good grades as you attend school, but never be the best. Do not draw attention to yourselves. Never run for any kind of office in school or as an adult. Do not join any kind of group unless it will put you in contact with those who need to be sterilized. Decide on a vocation that will put you in touch with as many addicts and their children as possible. It is a massive task, and you will only have the short lifetime of a human, which, as you know, is normally about 80 years.

As you are aware, there are fifty areas called *states*; three of you will go to each, and from the moment of your birth, you will have the ability to sterilize. You have studied each of the states for years, so you are familiar with the various goods and evils of each. We have selected your assignments, but you cannot know where you are headed. After your birth you must absorb all information and make decisions without preconceived ideas. You will attend their schools and sterilize every human in the school whom you determine to be worthless, both male and female. Even if you know that at some future date in his life, a human will change for the better/and become a useful citizen, you must sterilize him for fear that he may reproduce while still in a bad time in his life. You can't see everything in their futures, but you will have enough information to make a valid decision regarding whether or not to sterilize. We have to stop these destructive humans before their areas of habitation are overrun with danger. The other sectors will be watching each of you, and based on your success, they plan to institute their own programs of sterilization. In the past we have stopped severely damaging behaviors with disasters, but that method fails to allow the good to live. Once this program is terminated, the *Pleasures* will evaluate its worth and determine the next step in cleansing the Earth of many of the people creating perils for others.

You are all here because you have volunteered to perform a once-in-a-lifetime mission of kindness to the Earthlings residing in America. These people have a long history of trying to improve their knowledge, but they are greatly lacking in personal cohesion. They have begun to live separately from their neighbors and families, and their goals are becoming more directed at self rather than betterment of all and, ultimately, their nation."

Arania spoke up then and asked if they would ever be able to return to their homes.

"Yes, of course, you will return. When you depart from Star, you will go directly into the womb of a woman in your appointed state. There will be two women and one man assigned to each state. You will each go to a woman who is an addict in an area infested with addicts and drug dealers. Here you will be able to do the most good. You will all be born on the same day, at the same time, and will have the small, but noticeable star on your right hand so you can readily identify each other. In addition, you will have human, Earthly bodies and can die just as any other Earthling. In most ways you will be human, and can marry a human, but you can also get sick, so take care of yourselves. I cannot tell you what to try to achieve because each of the states is quite different and each has its own set of very complex problems. You must decide what you need to achieve as an individual, and do your very best to be successful. When you return, you will have an opportunity to share your experiences and your ideas with the rest of us. Good wishes and enlightened success to each of you. When you go through the portal that you see behind me, you will be sent directly into the wombs of the various mothers with whom you will stay unless some unforeseen situation occurs that would place you elsewhere. After you have sterilized everybody within your territory, you must find a way to move to a new area in which to search for those to sterilize, and so on throughout your lifetime. You must each make your own decision about your future on Earth. We can witness your progress, but we cannot interfere in any way whatsoever. Be very careful in these dangerous neighborhoods as we will not be able to protect any of you from harm. If you are killed, you will vanish, and there will be no body to examine. Naturally, your dust will find its way back through the portal, and you will come back to us exactly as you are today. The value of the mission is at stake, so take care of yourselves and live a long life."

The volunteers rose, made the symbol of their pledge to be successful, and disappeared through the entrance to life on Earth.

On Star, nine months is the same as on Earth, but never seems so as the *Starians* are always busy and pay little attention to the passing of time. They do not sleep, but they rest their minds and bodies for short periods in order not to miss new ideas. For the first time ever, however, nine months was going to be like a lifetime for the *Starians* who were the parents of the *Starlings who* had volunteered. They were in great fear for their children. Everybody had studied the element that the children would be sterilizing and they were so awful, so incredibly horrible, that they had begged and pleaded with their precious children not to go, but they knew in their hearts that they themselves would go if they could, as the situation was paramount to the total destruction of the country.

Frena, the mother of Arania, was devastated that her daughter volunteered to go, as she was convinced that she would never see her again. The *Starians,* who went to Earth in ancient times, died and had to remain on Earth. Supposedly, there was now a way to bring the dead back to Star, but Frena voiced her disbelief, based on the fact that it had never actually been tried and she did not want her daughter's dust to end up spreading through the universe. Her cries fell on deaf ears, however, for Arania had reached 200 and was allowed to make her own life choice without regard to her parents' desires for her future or fears that return was impossible.

Frena watched her child grow in the horrible woman's body. She was afraid she would be deformed or deficient in some way because of the lifestyle of the woman. As the time of the births neared, no mother would leave her home, but stayed tuned to her child every minute of every day. All would remain in front of the communication boxes until the death of their children. There was no requirement for them to be at their duties until their child was back home safely and securely. The fathers, on the other hand, continued to work and attended a monthly meeting to report to The Couple on the progress of their child.

As the children grew, the fathers gave more and more proud reports, prepared by the mothers, to demonstrate that the program was working, the children were safe, and the sterilization program was incredibly successful. One father reported that his four-year-old daughter, Deria, lived in the projects of New York and went through each building sterilizing every child, adult, and visitor she could get near. The count for one month was over 500. Pride was not a known emotion on Star, but that day, a father demonstrated just exactly what it was and how it felt.

The program progressed exactly the way it should have... until disaster struck. Arania was kidnapped and placed into a cargo box, in order to slip her and other girls past inspection. They were headed to China for various types of slavery. Frena saw it all as it happened and was out of her mind with worry. She begged The Couple to bring Arania back, as she could no longer do her job and was therefore of no more value to the program. The Couple invited Frena and her companion to come to their chambers for a meeting. Serena was the one who spoke.

"All of the Starlings who took this mission knew absolutely that we would never interfere. They could be beaten, held captive, hurt in many ways, but we would never come to their aid. The need for secrecy is paramount to success. Eventually, the Earthlings will know about us, but they are not yet ready. First, we have to rid the country of its present drug problem and let the righteousness take over again. Then, when they are mentally ready, we will meet with them. Doing so now would serve no other purpose than to alarm the entire Earth. They have many problems right now, as well as the lack of work that makes them feel good about themselves. The work they have always known is being sent to other countries, and we have to put a stop to that without infringing on another sector's progress with their country. Arania must save herself. She has already, just an hour ago, sterilized herself and all the girls in the cargo box with her. Do not be afraid; be content. Your *Starling* is taking advantage of every opportunity."

Frena was naturally both proud and heartsick for her child. It was almost more than a mother could bear. She sat in front of the communication box, watching as her precious Arania was used and abused, but she would never turn her back on her for one second. Her companion begged her not to watch, but she said that if Arania could endure the pain and humiliation, then she could as well. She would never leave Arania to suffer alone. As both companions watched, the crate with Arania and the other girls was loaded onto a shabby boat bound for China and the slave market there, and somehow the hearts of the parents knew that their Arania would never reach the shore. When the storm hit, the men threw everything overboard that was heavy in order to lighten the load and be able to ride the waves a bit easier. Seeing that the ship was in trouble, an inspection ship in International waters drew near to assist. Fearing that they would be caught with the girls aboard, they decided to throw their crate overboard. The penalty for transporting slaves was death, and since they could easily find more girls anywhere in the world, these 30 girls were just not worth the risk of being caught.

The girls were chained together inside the crate, making certain they could not escape or survive. With the heavy chains, the crate slid easily to the bottom of the ocean, completely out of reach of the inspectors. It would not be long before Arania returned to Star. They watched her die and ran as quickly as they could to the meeting place where the portal was located. They waited and waited, but no Arania. About three hours later, the Couple arrived and sat down beside them.

"It does not work. It works from Star to Earth, but something in the atmosphere has affected the program, and the scientists are unable to make it work in reverse again. We hoped by the time it was needed, they would have found the answer to the problem, but as yet there has been no success. They will continue to work constantly to see if we can bring the others back, but there is no hope for Arania. She cannot turn to dust underwater, and the ocean inhabitants will carry off bits of her body, when the crate opens, making it impossible for her dust particles to find each other, even if she surfaces."

Frena rose to her feet and hung over The Couple to speak. "You will have a transporter readied and go and get my Arania from the ocean, or I will go to Earth, as the volunteers did, and tell them exactly what we are doing and let them decide how to deal with the 149 Star citizens that are left." The Couple sat stunned as they had never heard of any citizen giving an ultimatum to any other citizen, let alone the leaders of a sector.

"You would not do such a thing!"

"Arania made her decision based on being able to come home, even though I know she never really believed that she would be able to return. She gave her life, but she can be saved, and you are going to order her rescue."

They argued and fought for half an hour until Frena ran to the portal and swore she would jump through if they did not save her child. She did not care if the transporter were to be seen; she wanted them to fulfill their promise and bring her child home.

"Her body cannot turn to dust under the ocean. She has to be brought to the surface to turn to dust, but even then, we cannot bring her home, because her dust has to reenter through the portal. We have never been able to collect dust and bring it back. You know that we have tried for thousands of years to bring our *Starians* back when they died on Earth, and we have never been successful. The portal is our only chance for the volunteers."

"You will use the underwater ships, put her on board in suspension and bring her home. She can be revived on board since she died underwater. Her body will not turn to dust underwater; therefore, we have a chance to save her. As long as she is not exposed to the elements above the ocean she can be saved."

With great difficulty they agreed. The Couple had never experienced a citizen threatening them or the success of a program. Frena would have to be disciplined when the rescue was over. If the citizens of Star discovered that The Couple gave in to a threat, how many others would put pressure on them to do things for their children to keep them out of harm's way, or to retrieve them because they were in danger? It was unforgiveable, and Frena had to be disciplined before the entire Sector 8. Nothing like this had ever happened in the known history of Star, and The Couple determined to see to it that it never occurred again.

The underwater transporter was dispatched to retrieve Arania. They cut the crate open and removed her from the others. She was placed on board in a secure suspension system and slowly, on the trip back to Star, restored her body, little by little, to its normal state. Dying underwater was the only thing that saved her. Had she died any other way, her dust would have scattered and never found its way back home due to the nonfunctioning portal. Even if her dust had made the trip, there was nothing on Star to give it direction, and it would have eventually dissipated around the universe.

When the ship landed, the parents were there to greet their Arania, showing emotions that they never knew existed within themselves. Afterwards, they were all taken to the area of The Couple where several *Pleasures* sat waiting.

They had reprogrammed the portal in anticipation of Frena's punishment.

"Frena, you have jeopardized the success of a major program, years in the making. You threatened The Couple, the first such action of which we are aware in thousands of years. You made a display of yourself not unlike that of the Earthlings with whom we are so concerned. You cannot remain on Star and pretend to be a citizen when, in fact, you are only concerned with yourself and your problems. There are 149 other parents who have been watching the horrors their loved ones are experiencing. Shall we give in to all their fears and tolerate their threats? What you have done cannot be overlooked or forgiven. Come to the front of the room."

Frena rose from her seat and went to the front of the circle of *Pleasures*, and with a swift movement, they hurled her out the portal. Arania screamed and buried her face in her father's chest. The *Pleasures* then turned to her and her father, who stood stunned and wordless.

"The Portal has been changed and Frena will not have a star on her hand, or retain any memory of Star. She will simply be born as a human, live as one, and die. She will remain on Earth and will never return to Star. Millions of years this planet has worked to perfect not only our citizens, in their bodies, but the ways they think, feel, and believe. Always, we work for the worth of every citizen in Sector 8. Selfishness and threats of any kind are intolerable. Arania has committed no crime whatsoever, so we leave her with one parent. Otherwise, we would banish her father as well. You had a duty, to your companion, to discuss her attitudes before she committed her crimes. You never reprimanded her actions or interfered in any way. You are not allowed to choose another companion in your lifetime, as you have demonstrated you are not worthy to be one."

The *Pleasures* turned their backs on him, a demonstration of their total disgust. Father and daughter departed, knowing full well that they would be viewed as outcasts until their deaths. No man would ever want to be Arania's companion, and all her father's friends would be polite, but would never again wish to be in his company. They talked for a long time and finally made their decision. They could no longer live on Star. Hand in hand they went to the meeting room and were grateful to find that the portal was still operating as it had for Frena. They kissed and hugged and gave their solemn word to try to remember Star and to find each other again, and to watch for Frena. Arania stepped through first, and her father followed.

The *Pleasures* came from behind the wall, patting each other on the back and giving great accolades to a family of such devotion and strength. They had hoped that they would make the decision to go to Earth, and had already programmed them into two very nice homes with very good friends and relatives. Their lives would be full of rich rewards of accomplishments. Frena, on the other hand, went directly to the slums and would never leave except by dedication and determination. They would be keeping a close eye on her and recording her every behavior, both good and bad, to use in the classrooms. This was an event that every *Starling* would study for centuries to come, making reports on what he/she would have done in Frena's place. Each had to be prepared for his/her own future, and had to be told the truth, always the truth, in order to know how to live.

Earthlings still did not understand that the residents of Star had visited Earth in the past, and many *Pleasures* remained, buried in various countries. They had come to Earth on a mission of mercy, to trade knowledge for minerals, but what could they trade for today? The Earthlings had nothing to trade for the knowledge on Star. The Earthlings barely had anything that one another wanted, except for land. Each country seemed preoccupied with overrunning another country for no other reason than power.

Perhaps one day, the leaders on Star would agree that it was time to reveal themselves to the leaders on Earth, but they knew it would probably be thousands of years away.

COUNTRY FOLKS

Billy Carter and Peggy Fenster became friends on the first day of kindergarten. As they were placed on the school bus, by their parents, they clutched hands and sat together. The first day for any child can be frightening, and even more so for children from the country who do not have lots of friends to grow up with. Billy and Peggy lived across the road from one another, but not being allowed to cross the road alone, they had never had an opportunity to play together. Coming from the same place, a farm, made them instant friends, and they stayed friends forever after.

The Carters had a huge farm that raised cows, goats, and chickens. The Fensters raised llamas, sheep, and chickens. Both children were intrigued with the chickens and accepted all the chores that went with raising and caring for them. As they grew, they naturally discussed their problems and ambitions with each other, competed in the local fairs with their hens and roosters, and both agreed that being a chicken farmer would be the best living life could offer.

In high school they went to the school activities together because no boy ever invited Peggy, and Billy never had any desire to be with any girl but Peggy. He felt that most of the girls were silly and vain, but Peggy was always just herself. Neither realized that they were building a life together because there were so many other things grabbing their attention as teenagers. As graduation approached, the serious talk of future began to creep into their conversations, until one day Billy told Peggy that there was a place she absolutely had to see. On the next Sunday, Billy got the old pickup truck, and off they went to see this wonderful place.

They drove for 30 miles before Billy told Peggy to get ready to be amazed. They could see a huge mountain in the background as Billy turned down a dirt road. As they continued, the mountain began to approach them as if just waiting for their arrival. When they were a couple of acres away, Billy stopped the truck and they got out. Laid out in front of Peggy was the most beautiful land she had ever seen in her lifetime. The grass was green and wildflowers were everywhere. Billy took her by the hand, and they walked and walked until they finally came to a little creek. It wasn't very deep, and they took off their shoes and socks and waded across. The water was clear and cool and made them both want to go swimming. Billy showed her the small waterfall coming down from the mountain, creating the creek, and then pointed out the larger area of water further down the creek where they could swim in the summer. He told Peggy that it was his dream to own the land and to raise only chickens and children, and he wanted her to do it with him. She was surprised, delighted, thrilled, and unable to speak. Just figuring the answer would be yes, he gave her the first kiss they had ever shared and asked her to marry him. She blurted out a *yes,* and they both laughed.

"Where will we ever get the money to pay for the land?"

"We both have education funds, and we will ask our parents to let us have that money for our land. Neither of us wants to go to college, and we have never desired to do anything but raise chickens; we don't need an education for that. We've been training all our lives."

With their minds dead set on their future, they went home, got both sets of parents together, served them some lemonade, and laid out their plans. After a great deal of discussion, the parents agreed. The land was purchased, and the children were married. Billy and the fathers built a small home for the newly married couple and once they could move in and get settled, the first chickens were purchased. Billy built the small shelter for the chickens and taught them to come home at nighttime. The chickens would roam free over the land during the day and return to the hen house at dusk. The rooster seemed to be working overtime, as the chickens were laying eggs in hiding and little chicks were forever showing up in the henhouse, which had to be enlarged to accommodate all the babies adequately.

After two years, Billy realized he needed to enlarge Peggy's kitchen, as he had married a natural cook and her meals were extraordinary. She was in charge of selling the eggs and kept very precise books. She was also great at trading and might come home with a load of wood in exchange for a load of chickens.

In the middle of the third year they ran into problems. Billy found Peggy crying on the kitchen table as though her heart were broken. He sat down to comfort her when he realized that she was not upset, but so overjoyed that she had laughed herself silly. He could not get anything out of her, so she just opened her hand and held out the bits of stone that glistened. Billy was beside himself and insisted she tell him where she had found the gold. Finally, she was able to calm herself down enough to explain that it was in an egg, and when she cracked others, they too held gold. Apparently the chickens were pecking at the sides of the creek picking up what they thought was corn and eating the bits of gold. Logically, it should have passed through their systems, but instead, it was going into the eggs. The biggest problem was that she could not sell the eggs if they all held bits of gold. Not only that, but nobody could know about the gold on their land unless they wanted folks to be trespassing or, even worse, stealing and killing the chickens and maybe even *them*. Gold was very dangerous. Gold made very good people go very bad very quickly.

They decided to sleep on the problem and try to find a solution tomorrow. It only took one evening for Peggy to discover a way out of the problem with nobody the wiser. She told Billy to start his chores and not to worry. She went into town, and when she came back she was all smiles.

"Billy, we are now in the omelet business. Unload all the small jars in the truck and all the boxes of food. I am going to prepare omelet ingredients, in a jar, and Marge at Marge's Diner is going to buy them all and call them Omelet Surprise, because nobody will ever know what's in their omelet until it is served. I won't always have the same ingredients for the omelets, so they will always be different. As I break the eggs, I will remove the little pebbles of gold and just store them in jars. One day when we have enough gold we will cash it in and build a really nice house and a huge hen house where all the chickens will have plenty of room to have their babies. So, what do you think?"

"I think I married a genius, that's what I think!"

And so the couple went forward with their work and their plans. The omelets became known far outside their little town and Peggy really had to work hard to keep up with the demand. She was surprised that she was making so much money from her omelets. Madge paid her $1.50 per jar and sold the omelets for $3.00. Peggy got the jars back washed and sterilized by the equipment in Madge's kitchen. The partnership was absolutely perfect for each of them.

On the tenth anniversary of their marriage Peggy had to break the news to Billy that the hens had stopped laying eggs with gold in them. She was still making omelet ingredients because she had gotten so used to it, but there had been no gold for several weeks. Billy decided that they should take a quick trip north to a large city, where they were unknown, and sell the gold. On the next Monday, both of the mothers came to take care of the chickens and the omelet business while the kids went on their first vacation ever for a week. Everybody was happy.

When they arrived at the gold exchange office, they were all grins and smiles. When they left, they were both in tears, mostly due to humiliation. The clerk laughed in their faces so hard he could not breathe and called a fellow employee to look and laugh as well. Billy had exploded and asked what was so damn funny; the clerk said it was fool's gold and what did Billy think the clerk was, a fool? Then they laughed even harder. Billy snatched up the box of jars and they left completely downhearted. All those years of hard work for Peggy, and what did they have to show for it? *Nothing!* Silently they started home.

They had been riding for about two hours when Peggy brightened up, turned to Billy, and told him how they were going to turn their fool's gold into real gold. Before they even got home, Billy stopped at Madge's Diner and Peggy explained her plan. Madge was delighted. Now they had a brand new deal. Peggy would make cute little bags of the fool's gold, and Madge would sell it as the Omelet's Gold, gold that is straight out of your eggs. It was an instant success, especially for the children. They all wanted to have gold that came right out of the eggs that went into making their omelet. Women bought some for gifts, and after four years there was no more gold to sell.

On the anniversary of year fifteen, they celebrated their beautiful little home, their lovely hen house, and their prize-winning roosters. Peggy said her gift would require Billy to do some more hard work and with the puzzled look on his face, she informed him that he needed to build another room, as well as a screened-in porch onto the house. They were having twins. Just when they had given up hope of ever having any children, they were going to mass produce! It was their very best anniversary.

And life begins anew, with children who do their chores, go to school, find friends, get married, and make their own way in life.

HOW MARCUS MET MAUREEN

Marcus was an only child, raised by two of the kindest parents a son could have. He never had friends because he was not a group joiner and far preferred the company of his parents, his computer, and the woodworking shop in the basement of his home. He went directly from high school to an accounting course at the local university, and, by taking his subjects year-round, finished his education in three years instead of four.

At age 21 Marcus lost his parents when a drunk driver crossed the median and slammed into their car. The man received only two years in jail, owing to the fact that he was the son of a State Senator everyone believed was destined for the White House. Marcus would never let him get there.

Marcus' parents died debt free with homeowners' insurance that paid off the house and a $100,000 insurance policy. Marcus had never moved out and was content to stay in the family home. He paid his inheritance tax and put the rest into his savings account. He was employed as an accountant with the Federal Government, and that would be the cover for his forthcoming crimes if anybody ever questioned his whereabouts or his honesty. He did not anticipate any such problems occurring, but a good strategy was to always assume that somebody, somewhere, at some time, might question him due solely to the fact that he did not socialize. With all that in mind, Marcus initiated the downfall of Senator Brightford and son.

If one is going to steal, the primary concern is to make the theft not look like a theft at all. For instance, take only a bracelet from a box full of jewelry and the owner will assume it was lost, taken by a maid, or one of the children due to drugs or something. When all at-home avenues are exhausted, the victim will begin to remember who was in her room during the last party, or who might have been able to get into her room. She will not rest until she discovers what happened to the bracelet. She never calls the police because an outside thief would have taken everything and left evidence of a break-in. No, she wants to discover the thief herself. Why create bad publicity that might affect her husband's future or his standing in the community, and what if it was a friend in cash-flow trouble? No, it is always best to keep quiet and solve the mystery herself.

In time she would discover that a girlfriend had lost a pair of earrings, and, try as she might, could not discover how they got misplaced or taken. Then another friend and another, none having gone to the police.

The evening would arrive when Senator Brightford would hold a little campaign party to raise large donations for his forthcoming race for reelection. Marcus made a list of places women would go, in the house during the party, and entered the premises one weekend when Senator and son were gone fishing. With no wife in the home, the Senator had ordered a room prepared for the women where they could leave their coats and freshen up in the adjoining bathroom. It was obvious the women would be in this particular room due to the little favors left on the dressing table and in the bathroom. Marcus picked out several hiding places that nosey women normally look. Some went into a dressing table drawer wrapped in a hanky, a couple into the medicine cabinet in a bandage can, and some in a bedside table hidden in a powder puff container. Only one area needed to be discovered, and every inch of the room would be torn apart until all the missing jewelry was discovered.

Marcus had a radio with a police band on it, so he would know the minute the police were dispatched to the Senator's home. He had the number of a local reporter, said to be malicious in getting a story, and he planned to call him immediately after the police were on their way. About 10:00 he heard the call that women were screaming and accusing the Senator of being a thief and the maid thought it best to call the police. Marcus quickly called the reporter and, with a smile, went to bed. The Senator would never worm his way out of this one, and there would be more scandal to come.

The Senator's son was accused of the thefts, but everything was returned, and the boy received only six months in jail. The Senator received sympathies from all his friends and, in sincere earnest, they donated large sums to his campaign. Marcus still had a lot of work to do to change the minds of the rich public, but he had planted the seeds of doubt, and now planned to watch the seeds sprout.

Along with his accounting abilities, Marcus had an IQ bordering on genius. He spent a great deal of time looking into the campaign funds and the Senator's private account. He was actually surprised to find that there were some inconsistences with the handling of the contributed money. He had not stolen much, but it was obvious that the Senator had his hand in the campaign till. Marcus decided that surely the Senator needed more than he had taken and ensured that he got what was coming to him. Little by little he siphoned off the campaign funds, and then with an anonymous tip to the reporter, once again, all hell broke loose. The word was out that the Senator had embezzled his campaign fund, money entrusted to him for his reelection. The headline was a thrill to Marcus, but he never let on to anybody that he was overly concerned. Nobody at work remembered that the Senator's son killed his parents, and he intended to keep it that way. Since he never spent time chatting with his peers, his misfortunes were never foremost in any of their minds.

Just as the son was leaving prison, the father was entering Federal Prison-for 11 years. His assets had all been sold to retrieve the money stolen. The police discovered that the money had been transferred to a Swiss account, but there was no way to retrieve the funds from that country.

The son had nothing to come home to because everything was gone. There was no house, no cars, no boat, and no money. He had only become a sophomore in college when he was arrested for the theft of the jewelry, so he had no education with which to get a job. He went to visit his father to find out if he had taken the jewelry for which he had been blamed. He believed his father when he said, "*No!*"

Jonathan began to wonder who would have had the most to gain by ruining his father and himself. There were opponents who came to mind immediately and several enemies his father had made on his climb up the political ladder, but nobody seemed the type. Had his father really embezzled the campaign funds? If so, then he probably took the jewelry as well. Temptation could become an overwhelming desire. He finally decided that his father was a thief, and had lied to him, causing him to spend six months in custody, which had ruined his life. The jail time for theft was a stigma that would hang over him his entire life.

In a few months Marcus began to think about Jonathan being out of jail and had an intense desire to see him returned to prison for another crime. He had never paid for killing Marcus' parents, and putting him in jail for anything would be better than letting him get off without punishment of any kind. First, he had to find out where Jonathan was working, and that was no harder than breaking into the probation files. "I don't believe it," he said, as he read the name of his employer. Jonathan was working for the new Senator Williamson, III, who was running for reelection. The senator had been an old friend of Jonathan's father and, with a sincere desire to help the boy, had hired him to be his campaign manager, in charge of the donated funds. Marcus thought about this situation for a couple of weeks, wondering if it could be some kind of trap. He whisked around in the funds, Jonathan's private account, and finally determined that everything was legitimate. He began to take small sums of money, but he did not put it into Jonathan's account. It just disappeared into the virtual world: $100 here, $200 there, and so on for over two months. Finally, the normal accounting was held, and the accountant discovered thousands of dollars missing. Naturally, the consensus was, *like father like son*, and Jonathan was arrested. It was all circumstantial evidence, but without his father and his power, there was nobody to help him fight the charges, and he went to prison with the same 11 years' sentence his father had received.

Marcus celebrated by dancing all over his home and sipping champagne. It had taken him a lot of time and trouble, but he had finally gotten them both.

After a few weeks of not having to plot and plan, Marcus discovered that he missed the thrills and excitement. When he came home in the evenings, he had nothing to look forward to accomplishing. He had no choice but to begin the game anew. Whom should he go after this time? There were a lot of bad guys out there, but he just did not know one as well as he did the Senator and son. Finally, he decided to become a thief, using his same tactic of taking only one piece of jewelry at a time. That seemed to be the only way that he could continue to be a thief, without involving the police, and taking a chance on getting caught. He desperately needed some excitement in his life and not having any friends, he felt thievery was a good substitute. He would never steal from people who seemed to be decent, but rather from those who did not deserve to be so fortunate. And that is how he met Maureen.

Marcus determined that he had to have a good reason to go after somebody. His parents would never have approved of his being just a common thief. Therefore, it was necessary to find a victim that deserved what he got. That is how Marcus found Douglas Stevenson of Stevenson's Parts. After a lot of internet searching, he discovered an enormous number of complaints filed against him for cheating his customers. Nothing could ever be proven, and he was never brought to trial on any of the charges made against him. Marcus discovered that all the charges were about the practice of Stevenson to short count all his customers. He sold thousands of different parts, but only items that nobody would bother to count. For instance, if an order came in for 3,000 bolts, the order was filled precisely as ordered, but after hours, the small crew came on and shorted every order. The bolts might end up as 2,500. Who was going to count every bolt received? This cheating had been going on since Stevenson went into business, and that was why he was so rich. Nobody was willing to testify against him.

Stevenson owned a mansion in town, a luxurious beach home, a home in Florida, 4 cars, and a yacht that could entertain two dozen people comfortably.

Marcus learned that when the family went to the beach, they took the entire staff with them. The only person that remained behind was Mr. Wrigby, the gardener. He kept an eye on the mansion and brought in boys to help with the lawn and gardens during the day. In the back of the gardens was a small cottage where Mr. Wrigby had lived with his wife until she died, and where he now lived alone. Marcus knew that a man his age would sleep soundly. What really protected the property was an alarm system, and he had acquired a unit that could search for the code and shut off the alarm before it began to wail.

At 3:00 a.m., when Marcus knew the Stevenson family and staff were gone, he went to the home, entered, and was about to disengage the alarm system when he discovered it was already off. Panic set in immediately. The reasons were limited. Perhaps somebody came home for some reason. Maybe the gardener came in to check out something and forgot to reset the alarm… *or* maybe a thief was in the house. That is, somebody other than Marcus. With caution he crept up the staircase and slid along the walls until he saw the faint beam of a flashlight. He crept in and hit the man in the back of the neck, which sent him to his knees. Marcus tied up hands and feet quickly, emptied the thief's bag, and put all the jewelry back into the jewelry case. He knew it was all in the wrong places, but at least it was replaced. He then picked the thief up and slung him over his shoulder, noting that he was very thin and weighed practically nothing. He figured the guy must really be down on his luck to take such a chance as to commit a crime in this house. It would not take the police long to catch up with him as he began to dispose of the jewelry. Taking one piece never brings in the cops.

Marcus reset the alarm, left by the front door, and carried the thief to his car. He tossed him into the back seat, noting that he was still unconscious. Driving directly to his home, he parked in the garage, lowered the door, got the man out of the car, went into the house, and placed him on a chair in the kitchen. Then he pulled off the man's hood to discover that his thief was a woman with the most gorgeous red hair he had ever seen in his life. The two of them just stared at each other without saying a word.

Slowly, Marcus pulled a chair out and sat down, never taking his eyes off the woman.

"All right Miss, start at the beginning and tell me just exactly what you were doing in Stevenson's house stealing his wife's jewelry."

"Like so many others, I lost my job, then my little condo and everything in it, until I found myself on the streets. I could not find a job anywhere, doing anything. I got so hungry that I resorted to theft. I'm not proud of what I was doing, but when you have not eaten a thing in several days, you become desperate."

"How did you manage to get into the house?"

"I saw the old man come running out of the house chasing a dog and waving his cane. I slipped in before he came back. I had hoped to find something to eat. I closed the door on my way in. I guess he just forgot about the house and the alarm, and I watched him go on to his place out back. I found the black clothes and hat in the woman's room and put them on. Then I began to take her jewelry when I guess you came in and knocked me out. And by the way, my name is Maureen."

"My name is Marcus, and I believe in doing first things first, and it seems our first task is to get you fed. I'm going to untie you so you can get washed up. Run away, if you like; stay and eat if you prefer."

Having become a fairly decent cook during his years alone, Marcus whipped up a breakfast for both of them so she would not have to eat alone. When they were finished, the dishes were immediately washed, dried, and put away. Then he directed her to his parents' room and told her to feel free to use anything she could find. Having nothing else to say, he locked up, cut off the lights, and went to bed himself.

In the morning, being the weekend and not having to go to work, he dressed and went downstairs to fix coffee, only to find that it was made and a light brunch-type meal was prepared.

"You cook?"

"Of course I cook. How do you think I ate for seven years on my own?"

They both laughed and then sat down to enjoy the food and the company. When they finished, Marcus got a second cup of coffee and began to quiz Maureen about her background and her education. She revealed that, like him, she had been an only child. Her parents were not as clever as his, and they left her absolutely nothing when they died. They had a lot of debt, and she could not even pay those off with the few assets they had. She left her childhood home with nothing other than a few keepsakes and her clothes. She had a job and was able to rent a tiny, ill-furnished apartment. After three years she finally got her condo. It was not much, just one bedroom and one bath, but it was hers. Her salary covered the mortgage, utilities, and food. There was little left for clothes or entertainment, but still she was happy. When her company closed, she was flung into the street. It would be weeks before unemployment and food stamps came through, and she was hungry right then. So, she turned thief.

Marcus put his hands together, under his chin, as though about to pray. "Maureen, I have an idea, and I would like for you to hear me out. I've never had a friend in my entire life, other than my parents. You are the first person I've ever sat down and talked with, and I enjoy your company very much. If you will be so kind as to stay here, and make this your home, I will happily pay for you to go to college so you can get a good job and feel independent again. I know how important that is to a person of your caliber. Before you even ask, there is no obligation on your part other than you treat my home as your home. I would hope you would do housework or yard work or just anything a person would do to take care of her home. You can clean out all my parents' belongings and call the bedroom yours to fix up any way you wish. If you desire to have dates, I prefer you meet them somewhere as I would not want them here. You, of course, want to know why I'm offering to do this. In my entire life, I have never done anything for anyone other than my parents, and I feel it is time I do something for someone. I have spent every waking hour getting even with the men responsible for killing my parents and have ignored everything and everybody else. Any time you find you are not happy, or wish to be somewhere else doing something else, feel free to leave."

"That is extremely kind of you Marcus, and I would be tempted to accept your offer, except for one problem. I would not be able to stand the thought of you out in the middle of the night getting yourself killed when a homeowner discovers you, or the police arresting you because they spot you at a home that is deserted. I would never be able to concentrate on my schoolwork. Besides, I would hope that you would be here in the evenings to help me study and to have dinner with so I don't have to eat alone as I've been doing for so long. How about it; can you hold off for three years? You did tell me that you could get me through college in three years, didn't you?"

Marcus said he was in no hurry to be a thief because he had a more interesting project staring him in the face just now. They began to make plans, to clean out his parents' room by sorting what was to be kept, what clothes and items should go to charity, and how the room should be arranged. He then took her to a ladies' store to buy some clothes and shoes. After dinner they made plans to visit the local university, the same one that Marcus had attended. Monday he went into work and took a two-week vacation, his first since beginning work. On Tuesday they headed to the university and signed up for her classes. Her deepest desire was to be a veterinarian, a secret that she had never shared with anyone as it was so hopeless. With Marcus' help, she knew she could manage.

On the first day of her first classes, Maureen secured a job in the library in order to help pay for her extreme expenses. She never told Marcus that she would pay him back, but secretly that was her deepest desire. A generous friend should receive some repayment for his kindness. The money she made went for groceries to make meals that would surprise Marcus. She bought little things to make the home cheerier, like vases for flowers, pretty dishtowels, and beautiful bath towels. Marcus was delighted with her little surprises and could not wait to get home from work each evening. He was having as much fun as he did when his parents were alive.

Maureen was delighted to have Marcus as a tutor. He was truly brilliant and gave her numerous ideas on how to remember information. With his guidance, she passed every course with nothing less than a B. She was amazed that she was able to do a good job on her homework. She had always been a bad student and never really understood anything she studied. With Marcus' help things seemed to make sense, for the first time in her life.

On Saturdays they began to go to activities like a fair or a movie, or just take a long drive to see the scenery and have lunch at a quaint restaurant. The years sped by, and Maureen graduated and began vet school. It was an extremely difficult course, and she had to work in a clinic. Both took up her days and nights. When she did come home, she fell into bed like a dead person.

While she was working so hard, Marcus was gradually picking up where he had left off when he ran into Maureen. In the evenings when Maureen was out, he would research his next victim. He continued to steal only one piece of jewelry and stashed his prizes in a little box hidden behind a loose board, under the stairs, in the basement. He always coincided his nights of thievery to his shopping trips. He told Maureen that he liked to grocery shop late at night as it took him a long time to make decisions. He read all the labels before making his choices and did not have the patience to shop with screaming kids and loud-talking women. He actually made his robbery and then dashed through the grocery store at top speed, grabbing things off the shelves like a lunatic. When he hit the register, he did not want one single person to hold him up. He figured Maureen would never be the wiser.

While he was on one of these shopping trips, Maureen was using his computer to research a paper, and stumbled across some of his files concerning finances stashed away in a Swiss account, along with the account number. She never would have used his computer, but she had forgotten hers at the clinic and, thinking he would not mind, had just started it up. In a panic she closed it down, but not before she had written down the Swiss account number. When he got home, she casually asked him if she could use his computer and he immediately said *no*. He told her that it was like using another person's toothbrush. They both laughed and she said she would be more careful in future about bringing hers home.

The day she graduated, Marcus gave her a little car, and she gave him the loveliest gift he had ever received in his life. She told him that she wanted to take over the clinic where she had been working as a training veterinarian, and wondered if he would like to be her partner and be in charge of the books. In the beginning, he would have to do it all: make appointments, answer the phone, pay the bills, and keep the accounts straight. He was so delighted that he picked her up, swung her around, and planted a kiss right on her lips. He was so embarrassed by his actions that his face turned red and he started to apologize.

"Good heavens Marcus, does it mean that you want to marry me since you just kissed me?"

Marcus stood there mute. Maureen grabbed him by the necktie and planted another kiss on him.

"I said can we get married now?"

"Married? Yes, married is a good idea. First things first you know. We have to get a license and rings, and I think we can marry in 2 or 3 days. Is that all right with you?"

"As long as we do it, it's all right with me! But instead of wasting money on a honeymoon, I want to just enjoy our home and get started on our clinic."

And sure enough, in 3 days they were husband and wife. They had gotten married at a Justice of the Peace at 10:00 am, and when they arrived home at 11:30 am, the house was full of policemen. Maureen was taken into one room and Marcus to another. Maureen told the policeman that she knew a wife could not testify against a husband, but as long as they found the jewelry themselves the theft charges would still be valid. They assured her that the charges would definitely hold and explained to her that he might be sent up for 20 years. She told them she did not care because she would be waiting for him no matter how long he was in prison. And after all, many really decent men get a parole after only a few years. They agreed that it was very likely he would qualify for parole. They understood how hard it was for her to see him imprisoned on their wedding day, but praised her for her honesty. She had explained to them, when she arranged for the search, that she could not live with a thief or tolerate it continuing. She had only discovered the jewels the day before coming to the police, and it had to be stopped. She would ask him to tell who owned each piece of jewelry and it could be returned. The police were in awe of this brave and honest woman. They had no idea that it was all a plot to become sole owner of everything Marcus had, and she kept the Swiss account information to herself.

Marcus was sent to jail and even though bail was set, it was never paid and he stayed in jail until his trial. He received 18 years on a Wednesday, and on Thursday the house went up for sale, the joint bank accounts were closed, and Maureen was on a plane to Switzerland. The account had over a million dollars in it, and she nearly fainted when she saw the amount. It had taken her 8 years to recover all and more of the money he had stolen, but it was all worth it. Marcus was not a bad sort and living with him had been fun, most of the time. She had an education and was a lot smarter now than she was years ago, when she was told that she would never marry Jonathan because she was not good enough for him. He did not stand up to his father, but just stood there like a little boy and let his father throw her out of the house. Now *she* was the lady and they were the trash to be thrown out.

Maureen did not waste the money, but used Marcus' rules to furnish the house and make it into a comfortable home. She then bought a large clinic, hired her staff, and taught everybody how to get and keep clients by giving the patients all the love and care they deserved. When the clinic was well received in the town and business was booming, she began to try to get Marcus out of jail.

First she had to explain to Marcus why she did what she did. He no longer had his parents' home, no money, and no Swiss account. However, he did have her and the Senator's house. What she wanted to know was whether or not he wanted to come home. He said he did.

Sitting alone in his cell, Marcus cried. He had done everything he could for Maureen and he had hoped she would find her own happiness without messing up *his* life. He let himself get overly excited when she wanted to get married. Had he taken time to really think it through, he would never have agreed to marriage. He wanted life to return to the way it was before he met her. He liked his quiet, ordered home, set routines, theft, and a large sum of money waiting for his retirement. He cried himself to sleep.

A few well-placed dollars got Marcus a pardon and Maureen was waiting at the gate for him, in a brand new station-wagon. She got out of the car and gave him a great big smile.

He slowly walked toward her, put his hands around her neck, and strangled her, right there, right then, outside the Federal Prison. He dropped her to the ground, turned around, and walked back to the gate. Without a word, they opened the gate, and let him back in, cuffed him, and called the local police.

SWAMP CHILD

The day Louisa Marsh turned five years old, there was no traditional birthday party with other children; in fact, there was no party at all. She could not be disappointed at not having a party because she had never encountered other children or adults gathered together to celebrate any occasion.

Her fifth birthday would be the same type of occasion as the other four had been, with a new addition to her learning experiences. She would now be allowed to leave the safety of the screened-in porch and descend the stairs to the large play area in front of the magnificent swamp home. The entire place was covered and screened to prevent the animals and bugs from ever getting close to this precious child. No expense had been spared for her entertainment and knowledge. She wandered around the space in which she would now be allowed to play and gazed at all the fascinating new things as each was introduced to her by her mother and father. Her parents demonstrated the swings and slides, badminton game, tennis court, and swimming pool. Louisa was extremely happy to have so many grand things for her physical and mental entertainment. Her parents would teach her how to play the games and how to swim. One of them would always serve as her opponent in the competitive activities, and intense notes would be kept on her ability to grasp concepts, as well as her competitiveness.

When Louisa turned six, she was given the opportunity to learn to read and write English, French, and German, which she did simultaneously. She had an astonishing ability to learn quickly and remember everything she had been taught.

At seven she began with elementary math and continued straight through to calculus. She enjoyed numbers so much that her parents had a difficult time getting her to put the books down and go to bed.

Age eight brought her the thrill of science, and at nine she began studying the history of the world. She was completely fascinated with the fact that countries would kill thousands of people just to take their land. She questioned over and over again, why people could not just be happy with what they had and let others keep what they had. The parents had no answers for her numerous questions.

When she began studying a particular subject, fabulous books appeared that made learning fun and added reality to the subjects. Not only was grasping information the first time she read it a sign of her genius, but she also displayed an ability to remember and recall anything and everything. Her brain stored every word read or spoken.

On the morning of Louisa's tenth birthday, she awoke to the loveliest sound she had ever heard in her young life, it seemed to float on the air, not like the songs of birds or the noise made by talking or walking, but soul-fulfilling melodies. She jumped out of bed and raced down the steps, and there stood her father grinning. Her father said, "Music," and Louisa turned to see her mother moving her fingers fluidly across the black and white keys of a piano.

"You will learn to play the piano yourself, but first I want you to hear some of the world's greatest concerts, and some different kinds of music written by people from all over the world. This box is called a *record player,* and these black discs are called *records*. You place a record on the box like this, pick up the handle that holds a needle and place it at the beginning of the record, and when the music stops, take the record off and play another. There are 100 records of all kinds of music, and you can play them all, in your room, for the next two days. Then your lessons will begin and you will learn how to play the piano. But, don't forget your school work. I don't want you to be so fascinated by the music that you forget to study. For today, since it is your birthday, you may have the entire day for music."

"Thank you for the day father, and I will not forget any of my lessons and only play my music in my free time."

Louisa felt that she would burst wide open at the various magical sounds that brought such happiness into her solitary life. Her father said that she would learn to make beautiful sounds herself on the piano and she was filled with a kind of joy that seemed quite new to her. Louisa knew that *people* had created these lovely sounds, and she longed to sit and watch them play. She had learned from her books that other people lived in other places and had something called *friends*, but she was never comfortable asking her parents why they lived alone.

Intuition is very strong in the minds of the young, and Louisa had always felt that there was some kind of connection missing between her and her parents. Even though she loved her parents, she never had a sense of the kind of closeness to them that gives a child the confidence to discuss feelings, and, so, she never told them how she felt.

That very evening, she asked if she could have her first lesson on the piano. She fully intended to learn to play like those who performed the music on the records that would take the place of the loneliness invading her little world lately. Her parents agreed, and she worked hard every day and learned to play the piano with the depth and skill that her parents knew she possessed. Recording her abilities always gave them great pleasure, as they knew her successes would ultimately produce great rewards for them.

One afternoon as Louisa was relaxing on a float in the swimming pool, she looked up at the house and began studying the windows. For some reason, they seemed odd. Her brain immediately began to calculate the floor plan of the house, and she felt something was definitely unbalanced. Her parents each had their own room, owing to the fact that father snored so loudly that mother could not sleep in the same room with him. Mother's room was next to Louisa's room, and the two of them went the entire distance of the hallway, but father's room was in the back of the house. She had been in her father's room, and it was not as long as the hallway. The number of windows in the front of the house did not match the number of windows in the back of the house. The windows for she and her mother numbered six, but father only had four windows. She could not account for the area next to father's room. In the hallway it was just a wall, but what was behind the wall? She could not help but feel the need to investigate, but something told her not to reveal her concern to her parents. She wrapped a towel around herself and went into the house to see where her parents were. She found them both in the living room looking at some pamphlets, so she slipped quietly up the stairs and entered her father's room, stepping into his walk-in closet to search the area at the back. Sure enough, she discovered a door that opened into a large room full of books and supplies. Many of the volumes she recognized, but there were some that she had never seen. They had very thin covers, and the pictures on the covers were very strange. She grabbed a few and fled to her room quickly, scared that one of her parents might come looking for her and catch her in the secret room.

Like children everywhere, she found ways to read these strange books and to keep them hidden from her parents. She had always been such a good child, doing everything she was told to do, that they never searched her room, or demanded to know what she did with her free time. She devoured romances, mysteries, science fiction tales, true crime, and all kinds of autobiographies and biographies. It would be from these books alone that she would develop a vast amount of common sense and an ability to devise and bestow a severe revenge on people that she had not yet even met, not to mention a fair amount of deliciously bad language. It was from these books that she discovered things that she had never seen: parties, radio and television, cars, boats, and airplanes. In every book there seemed to be something new and exciting, but she could tell that the writers felt that the readers already knew about and used all these things and, therefore, neglected to explain their exact appearances and uses to her satisfaction.

On the morning of Louisa's 11th birthday, she awoke before dawn, totally unable to sleep another moment due to excessive excitement. Today was to be her greatest birthday gift. She was going to leave the home she had lived in for her entire life. She was going to meet new people: children of her own age.

Finally, at 7:00 a.m., her mother tapped on her door and told her to get up, dress in the clothes laid out for her, and come down to breakfast. Inside of ten minutes she was at the table, picking through the scrambled eggs with her fork. Her parents both grinned at her and wished her a happy birthday.

"Today you leave the swamp and travel to the city to attend a marvelous school with other children. We will all be leaving right after breakfast. All of your clothes have been packed for the trip, but you must leave the books, toys, music, and record player behind so you will not have any distractions from your school work. Eat well Louisa, for it may be a long time before you have another opportunity to sit down for a meal, and you will grow hungry long before then." *School* intended that all the children arrive with stomachs as empty as possible, as their first shock would cause a great deal of nausea.

Louisa closed her eyes to keep from letting the tears flow down her face. Today would be a day of many intense emotions, and her world would be turned upside down. She was about to embark on a journey that would completely change her life. The first thrill of the day was seeing suitcases lined up at the door signaling they were surely going on a trip, giving her confidence in the promise that she would soon see other children. A man knocked on the door and hollered out that the boat had arrived, and Louisa nearly lost her breath when she saw her first new adult. Her mind kept screaming, ""There are other people out there, and you are going to see some today!" She wanted so much to act mature and not jump for joy every moment, but her knees threatened to give way, and her little fingers were shaking. She wondered if this was what the word *afraid* meant, an emotion she encountered in the secret books. When the knock and voice were heard at the door, Louisa ran to be the first one to see the new person. There stood a man much older than her father, and Louisa just stared and smiled. As Joe looked at Louisa, he fixed his gaze on her eyes…those storm-cloud grey eyes…so much like his son's… Finally, he shook himself out of his daze, said hello, and got the suitcases and the three people into the boat. The man's name was Joe Sawyer, and he chatted with Louisa as they rode through the swamp towards their destination. As far as Joe knew, nobody had ever come to the house in the swamp other than himself, when he delivered supplies late at night. He put everything in a metal bin on the pier and retrieved the envelope with the money and new instructions. He had been warned never to come to the house in the daytime for any reason whatsoever, so he had been amazed to find the details for his services today, early in the morning. He always assumed that he was working with some hermit who wanted to be isolated from the world. He never had a clue that a child was being raised in this house, nor that there was a wife. The groceries were always in a box, taped down securely, so he never saw the kinds of foods that would indicate a child's presence. When Joe came, in the night, he could not see beyond the pier. The play area was screened in, making it invisible in the black of night. Joe was never tempted to explore because the swamp is dangerous after dark, and one does not go into unknown territory when warned to stay away.

When the group pulled up to a small dock and the suitcases and passengers were unloaded, there was another new adult waiting for them. This man's name was Thurmond, and Louisa had no desire to be friendly to him. He was very big and looked very mean, all dressed in black and disregarding her as he gathered up their luggage and stored it into the back of a very long, black vehicle. Today, so far, she had ridden in a boat, and now a car that was probably called a limousine, another bit of "illegal knowledge" gained from her journeys through the secret books. Louisa had a feeling that those books had probably given her a lot of information that would be very helpful to her, but she was careful to keep quiet and let her parents explain about things and give her whatever information they felt necessary on this trip. It was going to be a lot of fun to see what she already knew. She remembered this vehicle from a description in one of the books, but it was a lot bigger than her imagination had allowed. After about 30 minutes, they approached an airport, and Louisa put her face right on the glass to try and see as many airplanes as she could. She wanted to keep track of everything she saw on this first day of her life outside the swamp. *So, this is what the books meant by having an adventure,* she thought. *I'm having my first real adventure!*

Louisa was entranced by the outside world and was disappointed when the driver stopped right beside a large airplane that her parents said was one of the school's private jets. She had hoped to be flying with lots of other people. With very shaky knees that threatened to buckle at any moment, she climbed the few steps and went inside. The only adult introduced herself as Sally and said she would see to their comfort during the flight. The first thing Louisa did, and in quite a hurry, was to go to the bathroom. Excitement was playing havoc with her entire system. When she returned, she sat by the window so she could watch the takeoff and the clouds as they flew. Sally handed her a glass and said, "This is ginger ale, and I think you will like it. This bag contains pretzels, and this one has peanuts." Three more new things just appeared in Louisa's life. What a birthday this was turning out to be. She sipped the drink, which did funny things to her nose and throat, and stashed the food in her pocket in case she got hungry as her father had warned her she might.

The noise of the plane warming up settled directly inside her stomach, and she was ever so grateful that she had been sipping the ale as it seemed to have a quieting effect on her insides. Instantly, the plane was moving down the runway so fast she was having trouble focusing on the objects outside. Then, her insides did flip flops as the plane left the ground. Even though she was afraid to look outside, she did so anyway. There were no words in her memory to describe what she saw and felt. Down below, everything was getting smaller as the plane headed for clouds of cotton. *Clouds of cotton* was a description she knew from one of the secret books, but she felt it was not adequate for the vision in front of her eyes. Then it happened without warning; they broke through the clouds and were now flying on top of them, as though they were carrying the plane through the air. She downed the last of her drink.

She tried to stay awake, but her eyes became heavy, and she fell into a deep sleep. Sally gave the parents the "thumbs up" so they would know that the sleeping powder had taken effect.

When Louisa awoke, it was at the touch of her mother telling her to get up. She was so groggy that getting up from her seat was a feat in itself. After getting off the plane and into another limousine, she slowly gave into sleep once again.

When next she opened her eyes, she looked out the window just in time to see the approaching "school" behind a very tall fence with barbed wire around the entire top. She was immediately frightened. This was not like any school she had studied. Excitement left her, and a low-boiling anger crept into her soul. The change in feelings was intense for the little girl, and she knew she was afraid. They passed through the guarded gates and stopped at the front door. They all got out of the car, her mother took her right hand and her father the left, to keep her from running away, and they entered the school together. Her parents seemed to know exactly where to go because they went down a hallway, turned to the right and then entered a small auditorium without so much as asking anybody how to get there.

When they entered the room, Louisa was surprised to see that the children were dressed exactly as she was, and she could feel that they were all afraid. They walked down the aisle and found her seat with the sign that said *Louisa Marsh.* Her parents told her to take her seat, place the card in her lap so that the speaker would be able to see her name, and be very quiet. They told her they were going to join the other parents in another room. In fact, they were going to a room where they would be brainwashed in order to forget the entire 11 years. They would never remember the swamp or Louisa Marsh. They would be programmed to have new names, new jobs, and enough money to make their lives moderately comfortable. For an instant, fear caught hold of Louisa, but each cheek was kissed by her mother and then father, and she felt more able to be grown up enough to sit here without her parents standing by. When she sat down, she gathered her courage and looked around at the other students. They were all separated by several seats so they could not talk to each other, but, of course, they did not know the reason for the separation. Each of them had simply been instructed to sit down, hold the name card in his/her lap, and not rise from the seat for any reason whatsoever. She counted the number of boys and girls, catching the eye of one little boy who looked petrified, so she smiled at him. She watched as two more families entered, left their children behind, and went to join the other parents, or so she thought.

It was another ten minutes before a man approached the microphone and began to speak.

"You do not need to know my name. You will simply refer to me as *Sir*. You will say *yes sir, no sir, excuse me sir*, or whatever the need to address me, but always as *Sir*. Every child in this room is eleven years old, well-educated by people I hired to see to your training for eleven years. They were not your parents, as each of you was kidnapped from families of genius. Your real father or mother or both were of such genius that it could be assumed that you are of a like caliber as well. If this news makes any of you cry or feel sad enough to vomit, look under your seats where you will find a bucket, tissues, and wet wipes. You may do so at any time during my talk, but you will do so quietly. You have all been raised without contact with other human beings except the adults you have called parents. The reason for your separation from the world was to ensure that you were not contaminated by information of poor quality or diseases of any kind. Never again will you see these adults." Several children reached under their seats. "Beginning today you belong to me. You will live in this facility and continue to train until you are 16. At that time, all girls will be sterilized and you will be transported to the underground facility where you will work until you die.

"Your teacher-adults have been reporting great progress, and I am anxious to see just how accurate their reports are as we proceed with your lessons. Enjoy the sunlight coming in through the window in your room, because once you leave here, you will never again see sunlight, hear birds, watch rain or snow, or enjoy any of the other outside pleasures." More buckets were pulled out for use.

"I have seen to your physical comfort and education and will continue to do so as long as you work hard and do not cause me any difficulty. For those with whom I am pleased, your lives will be as pleasant as possible, but for those who cause me displeasure, pain and grief will be swift. Since none of you has any choice in this matter, you would be wise to make the best of your situation and do as you are told at all times. The house where you were raised is already being torn down and the materials destroyed. In a month there will be no evidence that a house ever existed where you were raised." In fact, the books and toys had been removed and the houses were simply being sold. Sir would never throw money away, but the children had to believe that their entire existence was being eliminated. "I know that you may have developed a bond with the adults who raised you, but they were just doing their job, and you will never see them again. Once their memories are erased, they will never give you a second thought." Louisa touched her cheeks where the parents had kissed her and she believed they had loved her. She would never forget all the good times in the house of her childhood or the parents who so diligently educated and nurtured her for eleven years.

"You will learn that all children have a last name based on nothing more than a geographical location, not a real identity and certainly not the name of the people who brought you here. None of you has a birth certificate, and as far as the world is concerned, you do not exist. You simply belong to me. Tomorrow you will begin your lessons. On your name cards you will find a number which corresponds with your living quarters. Your suitcases have already been unpacked. You are now dismissed to roam the school on your own and find your rooms. Nobody will give you any assistance. I will see you at supper."

It did not escape Sir's notice that Louisa Marsh was the only child who did not move, did not reach under the seat, and whose beautiful face and storm-cloud eyes took on a fierce, dark look of total betrayal and hatred. He wondered what it would take to completely control her for her lifetime. It would be a shame if she had to be destroyed.

Louisa rose to leave the auditorium, and in an act of defiance, she reached under the seat for the bucket with the tissues and wipes inside, and left the room, swinging it carelessly back and forth, closely watched by Sir. She walked down the corridor as though on a sight-seeing tour, but her mind was set on finding her room the first time, without having to back-track. The numbers on the rooms were not in order, but were actually a math game. The digits on her card would be the room between 6 and 54. She had to figure out what number came after 6 and before 54 and that would be her room. She knew that 6 X 3 was 18 and 18 X 3 was 54, so her room was number 18. For her it was easy, but not so for many of the other children. They helped each other until everybody was in their room except the little boy that she had smiled at during the meeting.

In the forbidden books, Louisa had read about crazy monsters like Sir, but doubted that any of the other children had ever gotten their hands on the information she was equipped with and willing to use. She knew she had abilities beyond her years and she would never reveal her true knowledge or she might lose her advantage for escape. She would either get out of this horrible place or die trying. When Louisa entered her room, she was surprised to find that it was more luxurious than expected. A large bookshelf held all of the classics, and there were extensive sections on an array of subjects. While the general subject matters were known to her, the books themselves were all far more varied than those she had seen before, and they would afford her hours of pleasant reading. The piano stood in a corner just before a picture window that allowed her to gaze at the sky and the lovely garden while she played. She could not imagine that at age 16 she would never again be able to view the beauty of the outside. There was a chaise lounge where she could recline while thinking and reading, a bed large enough for several small children, two nightstands, and a dresser twice as long as the one she had previously, and a carpet so lush that it seemed to demand bare feet and toes for it to tickle. The bathroom had a tub, a separate shower, sink with a long counter, and commode.

The towels seemed as soft as clouds, and every possible hygiene need was supplied. She glanced into her closet and discovered that it was full of uniforms, but no pretty clothes like the ones she had growing up. She was already beginning to feel that she was losing parts of herself. Louisa's stomach turned as she remembered that no parents were paying for these accommodations, and the secret books said that *nothing is ever free.* She knew what Sir was really going to require of the students in repayment for all of these luxuries. They were going to work for him for the rest of their lives. It would be later, in the dining room, where she would discover there had been a great many eleven year olds brought to this school before her little group had arrived. Apparently, many had been here for a very long time and were now adults, and some adults seemed really old to her. She learned that children had been coming here during Sir's father and grand-father's time. A lot of babies had spent their lives in captivity. Apparently, the ones who were guards, cleaning people, cooks, and such failed to live up to the standards required for the underground facility and were put to work at the school. In the big facility, away from the world, they would need the same kinds of people to clean up after, and feed, the intelligent workers and to guard them to prevent escape.

Tears were hot behind her eyes; Louisa got on the bed, put her hands behind her head, and just thought about her situation. She did not move or cry out, but just lay there and let the tears slip down her cheeks. Louisa stayed in this position for an hour, silently reviewing all she had learned from the secret books. She realized that she had the advantage because of the forbidden books she had devoured, and she could call on this knowledge to help her survive...or cause havoc. Her

IQ had never been tested, but if tested, it would be the highest ever recorded, and this, coupled with her ability to recall bits of knowledge she needed instantly, gave her a real advantage.

There was an intercom in the room, and Louisa heard the announcement that dinner would be served in fifteen minutes. Any student who did not arrive within the time limit would find the dining room doors locked and would go hungry until the next morning. So...her parents had known about this all along, and that was why her father warned her about being hungry. She did not believe what Sir said about them not loving her because she knew they did just by the affection they had shown her. There was laughter in their home, games, teasing about wins and losses, and tender care when she felt sick. She would never allow herself to forget them. Maybe they did work for this horrible man, but maybe they, too, had no choice. Louisa got up, wiped the tears from her face, and made her own announcement. "I'm quite sure that you are spying on us, so pay attention; this is the last *damn* time you will witness tears on my face."

"Smart girl! Of course I am listening *and* watching."

"I guess that means I have to bathe and dress in the dark." Having said this, she picked up the bucket, took out the tissues and wipes, and container in hand, left her room. She already knew that her nose would lead her to the dining room. The bucket was to be used to steal food for anybody who might not get there in time and would find the doors locked. She knew there were equally 15 boys and 15 girls. She would count the children when they locked the door to see if anybody was missing. When she entered the room, a woman snapped,

"Name?" She answered and took her assigned seat. There was nobody her age there but her. She was stunned to see that there were children older than her at other tables. In a minute or two, here came another student. They were getting there one by one. Why not in small groups? Had she seen any students when she left her room? No! They were making the announcements a few minutes apart for each student and timing them to see exactly how fast they could react and arrive at the dining room without help from others. Had she known his stupid little trick in advance, she would have dawdled until the last possible moment, just to throw *Sir* off. She would certainly be on her guard next time. When the doors were locked, there was one boy missing. The supper was served family style, and dishes were passed around the table. When the biscuits arrived, Louisa took five. When the ham arrived, she took an extremely large amount. Without even trying to hide what she was doing, she made four large ham biscuits, placed them into her bucket, and covered them with a napkin. She then placed the bucket directly on her lap to prevent anybody from snatching it away from her, and actually hoped that somebody would try, because she was ready for a fight, no matter how badly she might get hurt.

During the meal, she noticed a girl much older than she watching her and smiling. A small kindness was much needed on this horribly scary first day, and she smiled back. When the meal was over, the door was unlocked, and as she walked into the hallway, she found the missing boy sitting on the floor with his head on his knees. She reached down, grasped his arm, and yanked him to his feet. Looking him in the eye, she said, "Never let them make you cry again, do you understand me?" He nodded his tearful face and, because she had a death grip on his arm, let himself be led away to her room. Once inside, Louisa put her finger to her lips to alert him not to talk. She took him to her desk, spread out the napkin, and put the four biscuits in front of the starving boy. He looked up into her face as though she had just become some kind of a god to him. She went to the little refrigerator that held milk and got a glass for the boy. The child ate for a steady 20 minutes and never spoke a word, but he kept looking around the gorgeous room. When he had finished, she wrote a note and he wrote a reply. This procedure continued until she had a solemn oath from him that he would assist in any plan she devised. She then tore up the notes and flushed them down the commode. Then, he wrote a note to ask her to help him find his room. He had been wandering the halls since they were released from the auditorium and could not figure out the code for directions. Math was his worst subject. She took the pencil and asked him for the name card that had his room number code. After a few moments she realized that there was no such number. Sir knew the boy was bad at math and had deliberately transposed the numbers just to confuse him. He was truly a cruel man. She took him to his room, and after making sure that he understood everything, she warned him again never to let Sir get the best of him. He hugged her tightly, and Louisa was shocked to realize that she had never been hugged in her life and could never understand what the word *hug* meant when reading her parents' books. She wondered if hugging had been forbidden by Sir.

Sir stopped her in the hallway as she was making her way back to her room and told her that he was shocked that she had learned a bad word and knew how to appropriately use it. He wanted to know just exactly where she had heard the word.

"All children are raised in complete isolation from any of the influences of the outside world. Where did you hear the word *damn* used?"

"I heard it from the man who gave us a ride in the boat. He hit his hand on something and used that word. I rather liked it," she said as she left him standing there and continued on down the hallway towards her room.

On the second day, over the intercom, it was announced that the schedule would be breakfast at 6 a.m., lunch at noon, and supper at 6 p.m. There would be no free time until after supper, at which time one could read, study, play music, or just sleep. It was absolutely forbidden for any student to leave his/her room during free time. No student was to be found visiting any other student's room. Isolation had invaded her life once again, and during these long years, the suffering would surely become unbearable. The only way she would survive would be to have a plan of escape in her brain. She knew in her heart that she had to stop this madness right now, but how could a child come up with a good plan? Surely many others had tried to escape and failed. How could *she* do anything?

Somebody was jostling her back and forth, but she was in such a deep sleep that she was having trouble waking. "Louisa, Louisa, wake up, it's your birthday!"

"What?"

"It's your eleventh birthday dear; get up and get dressed. Don't you remember that this is the day you will go on a trip to your school to be with other children?"

"I'm sorry mother; I guess I was just sleeping too hard. I'll be ready for breakfast in a few minutes, and then I would just like to walk around and say good-bye to everything. Will that be all right?"

"Of course you can dear."

This had happened to Louisa before, this distinct vision into the future, but she had never discussed it with her parents because she assumed it all came from the stories in the secret books. Something in her heart had always kept her from having the kind of trust in them that a child should have in her parents. From her dream of the future, she now knew why. And no, she had never been hugged or kissed. She dressed quickly, ate her breakfast, and dashed out the door. She hid just off the end of the pier, and when Joe came up with the boat, she ran to him and begged him to help her escape because these people had kidnapped her as a baby. Joe was old, but not stupid. He did not waste time trying to figure out if the child was telling the truth or not; he just put the boat in gear and off they went. If she was telling the truth, he was about to save a girl and make her true parents ecstatic. If she was not telling the truth, she would simply be returned to these people in the swamp. Louisa told Joe there would be a mean-looking man waiting for the boat, and he knew exactly where because he had received orders where they would disembark for the waiting limousine.

Joe went straight to his son, who was the sheriff of the swamp area. Sheriff Dan Rutledge was a no-nonsense man, but he had been raised in the swamp, had seen the house under construction, and always wondered why anybody would build a house of that size in that location. Surely none of their friends or family would visit them in the swamp. Now he would discover the truth. Nobody was ever allowed to visit the house for any reason whatsoever.

When Joe saw Louisa he nearly cried as he gazed into her eyes. He sat down and pulled the child close to him and asked her to raise her hair so he could see the back of her neck. He did not say anything to her because of the strain she was already in, but he nodded to Joe that this was his little girl who had been kidnapped 11 years ago. Getting hold of himself he asked Louisa to tell him everything as best she could. He was amazed that she started from the very beginning and in concise order told him everything he needed to know, in the order he needed to know it, so he could get help without anybody questioning his sanity.

Dan called in the FBI, the state police, and all the local police and had them converge on the school and grab every limousine that approached, holding driver, child, and adults alike. He had his officers pick up the man in black, Thurmond, and the people that acted as Louisa's parents. Warrants were ignored since it was certain that all the children were victims of kidnapping, and there was no telling how many children were involved.

Louisa was deeply concerned about the real parents of all the children. It was overwhelming to think of all those people underground, who had been there for years and years. Who did they belong to and how would their relatives ever be found? Nobody knew their real name. She began to cry at the thought of all the people who would go through life without knowing who they were. Suppose the children had been stolen from all over the world? Dan put his arm around her and told her that there were many ways to let people know what had happened and get help from everybody who even knew someone who had a baby stolen.

When the plane landed, they quickly got off and ran to the waiting police car, jumped in, and roared out of the area with the siren blasting. Louisa's heart was in her throat as the thought ran through her brain that she might be wrong about the whole thing. Maybe it was just a school after all. In fifteen minutes she would know that she had been the savior of 29 other children about to be trapped behind a fence and kept inside by guards until they were 16 and then sent straight to an underground area for life. She saw the school in the distance, and it appeared exactly as it had in her dream. She knew it was all true. The police had stayed hidden until everybody was inside. "The drivers have all been detained, as well as the flight attendants. The pilots were all hired, so we let them go," said an FBI agent.

With the FBI and the police guarding the perimeter, nobody was getting away. Sheriff Dan took Louisa's hand, and they entered the school. Louisa walked straight to the auditorium, and there they were: 29 children, all the so-called parents, and the lunatic doctor, all in the middle of total bedlam. It seemed that everybody was talking at once. Sheriff Dan was informed that a few of the adults were willing to tell everything for immunity, but the doctor was denying everything and the kids were becoming hysterical. Sheriff Dan walked calmly up to the stage, climbed the steps with Louisa still grasping his hand, and walked to the microphone.

Sheriff Dan yelled, "Everybody sits the hell down before I shoot somebody." The noise got a little less raucous. He took his gun out of the holster, and everybody immediately shut up and sat down. "Now, we know exactly what is going on here, so anybody that tells the FBI or the police forces a lie, even one, will have no chance at immunity. All the children are to come with me to the dining room. Everybody else will stay here and be interviewed by the FBI. Nobody is leaving this facility today without permission from the FBI."

"Sheriff Dan, I forgot about the adults who raised me. They are not here."

"Don't worry sweetheart; they are in my jail right now."

"Sheriff Dan, that boy coming towards us is the one I fed." The boy approached Louisa, looked into her eyes, and gave her a huge hug. It was the very same hug she had been given in her dream. My name is Thomas, and I saw you in my dream last night. I did not believe in my dream until right this minute."

The children went hand in hand to the dining room. Sandwiches and milk were fixed for all the children by a couple of police officers. Slowly, the other captives throughout the building came to the dining room. Within two hours the room was filled with social workers, the media, and doctors, who all agreed that the children seemed in good health but, now that they were being instantly exposed to so many people, would need to have their immunizations. The media was explaining to the public about the children and asking for all families that had ever had a child kidnapped to come to the hospital as soon as possible for paternity tests. The children were to be kept right there at the school where all the accommodations were already in place, and nobody would be able to have access to them because of the guards.

Two of the old people in the cafeteria told the FBI that they had come to the school from the underground facility. To the utter astonishment of the FBI they described an entire city. It was built for the purpose of having scientists work on various secret projects that countries around the world requested. Billions had been paid to Sir, Dr. Robert VanHausen, and his father and his grandfather. The city had been there for 150 years. They both knew where the elevator was located and the code to make it run. The entrance was behind an abandoned farm house and looked like nothing more than an old shed. The property was under heavy surveillance around the clock to prevent children or tramps from getting close to the elevator. Several hundred policemen descended in the elevator and shots were fired between them and guards for more than an hour to gain complete access.

Once they had everything under control, they found the intercom and announced that everybody was free and would be taken care of as they left the facility. Everybody was scared that they were all going to be killed and many hid trying to stay away from the people who invaded their world. It took an enormous amount of kindness to encourage people to come out of their hiding places and go in the elevator up to the world outside. Nobody had ever been kind to them, and the experience could not be processed in their minds. As they exited the elevator, the sun burned their eyes, and they all fell to the ground crying. Nobody had realized how daylight would affect their eyes, or their skin. Rescue was a nightmare. They were all told to cover their heads with cloth and the policemen led them to shade under trees. As soon as the buses came, they were loaded, and with the windows all covered, they were able to open their eyes. They could see out the window in front of the driver, and that caused everybody to start crying again. They were taken to a holding facility with cots set up, but there were so many people, that more facilities and more cots had to be designated for those rescued.

The FBI men and women walked around the underground city in awe. There were places for the workers to relax and enjoy the company of their peers. There was a game room, a library, a music room, and a gym. The bedrooms were all made up of just a bed, small dresser, and bathroom facilities. They all wore the same wash-and-wear uniforms and had nothing personal. Rules were posted that nobody was allowed in anybody else's room. The cafeteria and auditorium were large. The work room differed according to the space needed by the project. It made them all sick to think of the people who had worked and died during all the years since the creation of the nightmare city. It took a month for all agencies to agree to blow up the underground facility. No good could ever come from maintaining such a horrible place.

For the next two months, the kidnapped children and adults talked together, compared their lives, and wondered if their parents or relatives would ever be found. It was a very stressful time for each of them, and the decision to leave them together was brilliant because they comforted each other the way nobody else could.

Sheriff Dan came several times to visit the children, and especially Louisa. He knew that Louisa would soon know that he was her father, but he felt it best to leave her with the other children until she was ready to go. She was very concerned about Thomas and took good care of him, and he knew she would not leave until he was settled.

It was about three weeks before parents began to come to the school to get their children back. They all had horror stories about losing their babies and fell to their knees to hug the child they feared they would never see again. It was more difficult for the older children and older adults who had been there for countless years. Many were given opportunities to go to work for scientific agencies of the government while more research was being completed to put their lives and backgrounds together. One by one, many of the children left for their futures with a real family and real friends. Finally, Thomas' parents showed up and cried and cried as they hugged their little boy. At the end of two months, it was beginning to look as though the only person who might be left was Louisa. Sheriff Dan came to see her with a huge grin on his face. She already knew, but she let him tell his story.

"Twelve years ago I eloped with a very rich young lady, and when we finally told her parents about it, we were immediately made to sign an annulment. Her mother and father were livid that she would marry a swamp sheriff instead of a man of wealth and power. She never told me that she was pregnant. They are a very religious family so no abortion was even considered, and the baby was born. The night after the baby arrived, she was stolen from the hospital nursery. Your mother called me for help in finding you, and told me that you have a violet on the back of your neck, just like she does. I have searched for you all these years, and I knew you were my child from the first day you came to me with the strange story about this school. I had to wait for the paternity test in order to take you from here. I've always known where your mother was and I called her and gave her the wonderful news. She has never married and has grieved over you and me all these years. We are getting married again, and this time her parents have agreed, because it is finally obvious to them that we will never love anybody but each other." Louisa just sat there grinning.

"You look silly just sitting there grinning like that. Aren't you going to give your old dad a hug?" She flew into his arms and kissed his cheeks a dozen times. A hand touched her arm, and when she looked up, a beautiful woman was smiling at her.

"Please tell me you are my mother."

"Yes, love, I am your mother, and now that I have the two people I need most in this world, my life is finally worth living. Because of my brilliant daughter, so many families have been brought together again, and so many people who thought they would die underground are happy and free. I am so proud of you my child." Mother and daughter hugged away the lost years.

"Are we going to go back to the swamp to live?"

"No, my baby, we are not," said Dan.

"You and I are not quite like everybody else," said her mother. "Dan never really understood about my family being extremely religious. Our religion is not exactly like that of most people. Ours is total obedience. My parents bought our passage to earth with my first born child, and when you were stolen, it meant that we could lose our right to stay here on earth. We were allowed to stay on their promise that I would have another child by age 40, but I have refused to have a child unless I have permission to marry Dan, not one of my own kind or some wealthy Earthling. My terms were finally accepted, after all these years, because I lost you, but here you are to save the day, for *your* family, and many other families.

Our religion requires our complete dedication to all promises, debts, and agreements of any kind. My parents have obtained permission, from my planet, for me to marry Dan if I will keep their agreement to give up my first born child. You are very special and highly desired for study by my people, and that is why they have agreed to my marriage. I'm sorry, my love, but you will be leaving this evening, for *my* planet, to keep my parents' promise."

Before Louisa could scream, Dan injected a solution into her arm that allowed her to see, hear, and walk, but she could not speak. The three of them just walked hand in hand out the door like a loving family, on their way to a life that most people take for granted.

And, once again, Louisa was headed for an adventure.

CPSIA information can be obtained at www.ICGtesting.com
Printed in the USA
BVOW071506100313

315093BV00001B/3/P